BLL

D0376183

A.G.	_____	MLW	_____
A.L.O.	_____	Mt.Pl	_____
Ans	4/08 _____	Nor G	_____
Bad	_____	NLM	9/04 13/03 _____
Bev	_____	Ott	_____
C.C.	_____	PC	_____
C.P.	_____	PH	_____
Dick	_____	P.P.	_____
ECN	7/08 _____	Pion.P.	2/05 _____
ECS	7/08 _____	Q.A.	_____
Elm	_____	Riv	_____
Gar	_____	Ross	_____
G.H.	_____	S.C.	_____
GSA	_____	St.A.	_____
GSP	_____	St.J	_____
G.V.	_____	St.Joa	_____
Har	_____	St.M.	_____
JPCP	_____	S.L.	_____
Jub	_____	Sgt	_____
KEN	_____	T.H.	_____
K.L.	3/62 _____	T.M.	_____
K.M.	3/04 _____	T.T.	8/01 _____
L.H.	_____	Ven	_____
Lyn	_____	Vets	_____
L.V.	mcK 12/01 _____	VP	_____
McC	_____	Wat	_____
McG	_____	Wed	_____
McQ	_____	W.L.	_____
M.L.	_____		_____
Marshall	_____		_____
	_____		_____
	_____		∞

MACE'S LUCK

Detective Chief Superintendent Mace
has planned a perfect vacation in
California with his girlfriend, police-
woman Victoria Bercovici. But, shortly
after their arrival in the Napa Valley,
someone tries to kill Victoria. Soon
Mace and Victoria discover that the
rolling countryside hides a web of
deceit, corruption and crime. Worst of
all, concealed beneath the affluent
surface are long-buried hatreds and
the crazed mind of a mass-murderer.

JAMES GRANT

MACE'S LUCK

Complete and Unabridged

LINFORD
Leicester

First published in Great Britain in 1985

First Linford Edition
published 2001

Copyright © 1985 by James Grant

British Library CIP Data

Grant, James, *1933* –
   Mace's luck.—Large print ed.—
Linford mystery library
1. Detective and mystery stories
2. Large type books
I. Title
823.9′14 [F]

ISBN 0–7089–5986–5

Published by
F. A. Thorpe (Publishing)
Anstey, Leicestershire

Set by Words & Graphics Ltd.
Anstey, Leicestershire
Printed and bound in Great Britain by
T. J. International Ltd., Padstow, Cornwall

1

The motor-cycle cop came out of nowhere, the way that motor-cycle cops do the whole world over. He tweaked his siren and I pulled obligingly to the side.

I watched him in my rear-view mirror as he leisurely dismounted, propped the bike and strolled towards me peeling off heavy black leather gauntlets. It was quite a performance. If I hadn't seen it before in a thousand Hollywood movies I would've quaked in my shoes.

I yawned, catching sight of myself in the mirror. I looked as if I had driven about a hundred miles through fog immediately after stumbling blearily off a transatlantic flight. Which was not at all surprising as that was exactly what I had done. More than half a day ago I said goodbye to Manchester airport, thankful to be lifting out of thin drizzling rain and looking eagerly forward to many things, among them Californian sunshine even if that was a poor second to my principal reason for the trip. Since landing at San Francisco I had taken a crash-course in left-hand driving as I fought my way through heavy traffic before running into thick, rolling, yellow-tinged fog which was making me late for a very important date.

I was less than pleased with the world and the cop would not help matters but, then, I suppose he was only doing his job. If that was the case then I was the last person to complain.

He had reached me now and lowered his black and white helmet towards my window. I wound it open a crack and tried not to breathe too deeply as the fog coiled in; at the same time I turned down the radio. Peggy Lee's voice melted into that heavy silence peculiar to foggy days.

'Is this your car?'

'It's rented,' I told him.

'A San Francisco company.' It was a statement not a question, which proved he had read the licence plate.

I smiled and agreed. One thing being a policeman teaches you is to be polite to policemen.

'One of your tail-lights is out,' he added.

I turned off the motor, then opened the door gently, so as not to hit him, and climbed out creakily. Crouching over a steering-wheel and peering into fog is not the best way to recover from an eleven-hour flight. He told me no lies; I was short one tail-light. 'Sorry,' I said. 'I'll have it fixed in Calistoga.'

'That where you're headed?'

I nodded.

'This isn't the straightest way from 'Frisco.'

'I missed a junction in the fog and was in Winters before I could risk turning.' I could have told him that my caution had been due in part to the truck drivers roaring past me as if it was bright and sunny but I didn't. There are cowboys on the East-Lancs motorway too.

The cop nodded judiciously. 'Okay,' he said. 'On vacation or business?'

'Vacation.'

'From England, right?'

I grinned. 'The accent, I suppose.'

He almost grinned back but it might

have hurt the macho image. 'Something like that.'

I could see that beneath the crash-helmet, the snappy uniform with its razor-edge creases, the black leather gauntlets and high, shiny boots there lurked a very young man.

I waved a hand into the murk. 'I'm told this is a pretty part of the state. If this stuff ever clears, maybe I'll see for myself.'

'It is, and you will. The fog's due to clear in about an hour.' He made it sound as if he was in direct communication with the weather god. 'The guy on TV said so,' he added, confirming my suspicion that he had communed with a deity.

Engine noise rumbled closer and a heavy tanker truck nosed cautiously out of the fog. This was one driver who wasn't practising for the Indy 500. The cop waved the driver past us. White letters painted on the truck's side ended with 'onne' but I missed the rest. A decorative logo blended grapes and a glass which didn't need any deductive powers to hint that the truck's contents were Californian wine. With luck, I might sample my share soon.

'I'm low on petrol,' I said. 'How far is the next filling station?'

'Nothing between here and St Helena,' he told me. 'Always assuming you mean gasoline.'

'I mean gasoline,' I confirmed.

'You can have your tail-light fixed there,' he said as he turned towards his bike. 'Have a nice day,' he added, doing his bit towards cementing Anglo-American relations with the all-American, all-purpose farewell.

I climbed back into the car, mentally confirming that was exactly my plan. When I finally reached Calistoga I would have a very nice day indeed. The cop roared off, disappearing in a yellow swirl of fog. I started the motor, turned up the radio and pulled back onto the road. Peggy Lee had given way to a big band; Ellington, around the early fifties. It was an improvement on Radios 2 and Merseyside, one of which usually accompanied me around my patch.

If I hadn't been moving so slowly I

would have missed the sign. It was faded, collapsing, but was definitely pointing off to the right with the assurance that a mile down a side road I would find gasoline. I had taken the rental car over from another motorist before the agency had time to top up the tank, planning on managing that little chore myself. Now, the needle was flickering on red. Unsure how far it was to St Helena, I turned right.

Bouncing down a potholed road that hadn't seen a resurfacing gang in ten years, I guessed I had made a mistake. I wouldn't find a neon-lit filling station down here and, anyway, the young cop had assured me that St Helena was the nearest refuelling stop.

Ellington's 'A Tone Parallel to Harlem' came to an end just about the moment I reached another sign almost as indecipherable as the first. I was entering the township of Vidal. From what I could see in the murk the word town was outrageous hyperbole. Vidal was a falling-down jumble of houses, mostly timber, from which the paint had long since peeled. Perhaps the gardens had once been neat; now, leggy climbing plants scrambled up over walls, sagging rooftops and crazily tilting chimney-stacks. In the fog, which seemed whiter now, it looked like the set of one of those creepy old movies about things that go bump in the night. I wouldn't have been at all surprised if John Carradine had loomed out of the gloom. Everywhere I looked, windows were boarded over. One building, bigger than its fellows, boasted a weatherworn sign which announced that it was a hotel with first-class accommodation. Like the houses around it, the hotel's windows were boarded up. Even Norman Bates would have been hard-pressed to make a living here. It looked as if my guess was right and all I'd done was waste two miles-worth of fuel.

I slowed, searching for a place to turn. It was then I saw the filling station. This too looked like something from an old movie but not just any movie. It was a ringer for the set of *The Postman Always Rings Twice*; not the remake, the one with John Garfield and Lana Turner. I was using its forecourt to turn when the door to the adjoining diner opened and a man came out. I stopped, surprised that this wasn't a ghost town after all.

He was burly and round-shouldered, and walked with an odd set to his upper body. He leaned in at the window and asked, 'Lead-free or regular?'

I hadn't expected anything, let alone a choice. 'Lead-free,' I told him.

He walked around the back of the car, opened up the tank, then banged at various levers on an antique pump. I climbed out and took a closer look at him.

He was about seventy, dressed in a faded green cover-all that was stiff with oil and grease. He wore a matching green baseball cap, its peak pulled over a face that was seamed with thousands of tiny lines from among which small but bright blue eyes gleamed out at me. He had only one arm, the right sleeve of his coverall being knotted up at shoulder level, which accounted for the way he moved.

'I didn't think anyone lived here,' I said.

'Then why'd you come?' he asked, reasonably enough.

'I saw a sign up on the highway and took a chance. I'm low on pet . . . gasoline.'

He studied my face for a moment while the pump grumbled. 'You from someplace to the east?'

'That's one way of putting it. I'm from England.'

'Well, now, is that right? England.' He nodded, as if pleased at some kind of discovery. The pump made a noise like a man pulling a rubber boot out of a swamp and stopped pumping. The old man kicked the base of the unit. After a protesting gurgle, fuel flowed once more. Eventually, a bell tinkled and he returned the nozzle to its holder, hooking it in place with a loop of twine. 'Come on inside,' he said, turning away before I could argue. 'I have something that will interest a man from England.'

Inside, the building looked worse than it had from outside. The walls were close-boarded and maybe half a century ago someone had papered them over.

9

Now, the paper was split along the joins in the boarding and hung in looping threads down towards the floor which was covered in torn, heel-scarred linoleum.

The room was littered with a handful of tables and chairs and over against one wall was a counter that obviously served as a bar. Obvious because half a dozen unwashed glasses and a couple of empty beer bottles stood on it.

The old man pointed. On one wall was a framed painting of some kind, maybe two feet square. 'You ever hear of a place in England called Openshaw?' he asked.

'Openshaw? Near Manchester?'

He nodded, his expression curiously eager.

'Yes, I know it. My first wife lived there before we were married.'

He beamed at me, the creases in his face trebling as his eyes vanished momentarily. 'Take a look,' he invited.

It wasn't a painting, not exactly. It was a nineteenth-century certificate of apprenticeship, confirming that a certain William Haigh had completed his indentures as a wheelwright in 1872. The certificate was

10

covered in spidery curlicues, some ending in little ovals inside which were painted tiny portraits. One, a stern individual with muttonchop whiskers, was clearly the master; another, a fresh-faced young man, I took to be William Haigh.

The old man jabbed a heavy finger at the portrait of the apprenticed William Haigh. 'My grandfather,' he said. There was pride in his voice.

'Well, I'll be . . . '

We studied the certificate in silence.

'Time for a beer?' the old man asked.

Thanks to the fog I was already late, but this didn't seem the moment to be churlish. 'Sure.'

He went behind the counter and rattled around among some bottles. 'The goddamn icebox is busted,' he told me as he banged a couple of beers on the counter top.

'That's okay, we don't drink it too cold in England.'

'So I heard,' he said with a grin. 'I guess it takes all sorts.' He whipped the caps off the bottles before handing one to me. He raised the other. 'Cheers. Isn't that what you say?'

'Cheers,' I concurred.

It was early in the day, even for a working detective, but the beer tasted good and the residue of my plastic airline meals receded. Neither of us spoke for a moment.

'How many people live here?' I asked eventually.

He leaned an elbow on the counter and took off his baseball cap. He was completely bald, his scalp stained with the sun and marks of age. 'Day before yesterday there was twenty-two.' Something twinkled in his eye. 'But I ain't counted 'em today.'

We sank a few more beers and I told him about Openshaw, doing my best to make it sound better than it is by ignoring what had happened to the place since his grandfather left more than a century ago.

In return he told me about Vidal and how he owned just about every piece of it as the townspeople sold up and left to better, brighter things. The mining had long since ended and the soil was wrong for grapes and, anyway, there was more money to be made punching time-clocks in Napa Valley wineries or Sacramento industrial plants or making computers just about everywhere.

'How do you make a living, if there's no one around here much?' I asked.

'People come down through the summer. The lake's new. In the old days we didn't have even that.'

'Fishing?'

He nodded and pulled back the curtain on the window behind him and sunlight poured in. It looked as if the young cop's weather forecast had been right. 'The lake shore's only half a mile away,' he said.

I checked the time. 'I must go,' I said. 'I was late even before I got here.'

'Where're you headed?'

'Calistoga.'

'Nice town. You been there before?'

'No, but I hear it's a good place for a vacation.'

'This would be better. If I ever fix up the hotel.'

I finished off my beer.

'Come back this way if you have the time,' the old man said.

'I'll do that, Mr Haigh,' I told him as we went out into the bright sunlight.

'Call me Bill.'

'Like your grandfather.'

'And my father.'

'My name's Mace.' We shook, using our left hands. 'What happened?' I asked.

'I was in a fight one time.' He grinned again. 'You should've seen the other guy.'

I paid him for the gasoline and he refused to take anything for the beers. In the car, I waved farewell as I started up and headed back the way I had come. As I passed the boarded-up hotel I glanced back, catching a glimpse of the lake. I stopped and opened up a Rand McNally. Although I could see only a small corner of it, the map told me that Lake Berryessa stretched almost thirty miles northwards running up past St Helena and Calistoga both of which were located on County Highway 128, the road I had left to come down into Vidal.

I checked the mileage. I could make Calistoga in about an hour if I bent the speed limit but even so I would be more than three hours late. I drove up the road and out of Vidal.

As I passed the sign marking the town's limits I checked the rear-view mirror. Something reflected the sun and I made out a motor-cycle half-hidden among trees by the roadside. Sitting on the bike was a cop. It could have been any cop but I was sure it was the same one who had stopped me on the highway. The one who had told me there was no place I could buy gasoline this side of St Helena. It couldn't have been because he didn't know about old Bill Haigh; a cop knows everything that happens on his patch. Maybe he had an interest in the filling station he had directed me towards, maybe he didn't like Bill, maybe it didn't matter. If that was so, why was he hiding? I shrugged my thoughts away. I was here in California on holiday, and for another, much more important reason. Just because I was a policeman back home in Liverpool didn't mean I had to question everything that happened to me here.

2

Calistoga was everything I'd been told it was. Peaceful and sun-soaked, it even looked friendly from behind the wheel of a car which isn't something many towns achieve.

I parked outside the Mount View Hotel, angling the car in between a cream and white Winnebago camper and a mean-looking metallic-gold Charger. The hotel was painted a light sand colour with windows and mouldings picked out in blue. Above a decorative parapet a Union flag hung motionless in the midday heat. Take away the cars and TV antennae and it could have been a scene from a B-Western.

Heaving my bag out of the car I resisted an impulse to walk like Randolph Scott and went inside to cool darkness. When my eyes readjusted I crossed to the slim, dark-haired desk clerk whose name-tag told me he was Phil Smeeton. I introduced myself.

'Room 37. Mr Mace,' he told me. 'Your wife checked in last night.' His smile had a slightly wistful quality. I could guess why. I thanked him, choosing not to tell him we were not married because it wasn't any of his business and, anyway, we might soon end up that way. I went up the stairs, found room 37 and rapped softly against the door.

'Who is it?'

Her voice was exactly the same as I remembered. Of course, we had talked on the telephone a few times in the past ten months but that had hidden the husky, promising thrill. I told her who it was.

I didn't hear her cross the floor but the key turned in the lock. I stepped inside to hazy blue as sunlight filtered through a fully-drawn turquoise blind. The door snapped shut and something cold and metallic pressed against my neck. My mouth went dry.

'You're late,' she said.

'I'm sorry.'

'Turn around.'

I did as she ordered. The cold metal

was no more lethal than the room-key.

'That was unkind,' I told her. 'I just aged ten years.'

She smiled and I shed the decade faster than I'd put it on. Then I took my eyes from her face, looking downwards. Even if she had been wearing a suit of chain-mail my temperature would have doubled. As she was, completely naked, my blood boiled.

'Expecting company?' I asked.

'You're late,' she repeated.

'After ten months, what's three hours?'

'After ten months, three hours is one hundred and eighty minutes too long, you bastard.'

I smiled.

'Do you plan on standing there another three hours?' she asked.

'With a view like this. I can think of worse things to do.'

'And I can think of better.'

Her hair was longer than I remembered, hanging partially forward over her breasts, the dark brown contrasting with her lightly tanned skin. I couldn't see the chestnut highlights in the dimness of the room but I knew they would be there.

I touched her cheek with my fingers and then we were wrapped in each other's arms tightly enough to make breathing a problem.

I moved my hands so that I could ease her face away from my shoulder. Her dark eyes reflected more light than they should have done. 'Why are you crying?' I asked.

'For God's sake, Mace, you haven't learned much in the past ten months, have you?'

'About women? No. A monk would've had a better time than me.'

'That wasn't what I meant and, anyway, you don't have to declare your celibacy. I hadn't expected anything else.'

I began taking off my clothes, trailing them behind me as I headed for the bathroom door. 'It's been a long, hot day,' I said. 'Don't go away.'

'As if I would,' she said, and followed me.

Standing under the shower with Victoria I could feel tiredness slipping away together with the emptiness of the months we had been apart.

I had come to California the previous summer, hoping for a well-deserved holiday. Sidetracked into a trail of violence and murder, out of nothing more than an attempt to do a favour for an old friend of mine back in England, it had proved anything but restful. Only one good thing had come out of my adventure in Los Angeles; well, two, if you count the fact that despite all the killings I had saved my old mate's young daughter from a fate far worse than the fate worse than death.

The best thing was that the LA cop assigned to the case was Lieutenant Victoria Bercovici.

Since my return to Liverpool we had written regularly and telephoned occasionally but this was our first chance to be together again. A Detective Chief Superintendant in CID cannot take leave just when he feels like it, and I had certainly felt like it. And Victoria's efforts in the case we had worked on, despite being decidedly unorthodox, had resulted in her being upgraded and equally unable to take time off when she chose. This was the first time we had been able to fix leave simultaneously. She had wanted to come to England, but May promised to be wet and windy and so I talked her into agreeing that I should come to California. After all, as I pointed out to her, on my previous visit I had seen little of the country. In fact, once the murder case was wrapped up all I had seen was the inside of a string of motel rooms in which each of us had explored the pleasures of the other's body like a couple of teenagers who have just discovered sex.

Long before I reached out to turn off the shower, we had begun again where we left off all those months before.

By the time we reached the bed I knew I would have problems in making this last as long as I wished, but Victoria didn't seem to care. Maybe she felt the same, maybe she knew how I was feeling and didn't want to lay down rules I couldn't hope to keep. She wrapped her slender legs around me as we settled back on the bed, expertly rolling over so that she could look down on me. She smiled, then closed her eyes and, still smiling, began a gentle rocking motion as she lowered herself onto me.

As I entered her body, her moist warmth drawing me inwards, she sucked in a deep breath then let all the air out in a long sigh. 'I've dreamed of this every night,' she said softly.

'So have I.'

'Have you, Mace? Or are you just saying the words?'

I lifted my head from the pillow, momentarily taking one of her dark brown nipples between my lips. She sighed softly, her mouth curving in a smile of satisfaction. 'I'm not just saying the words,' I told her.

Victoria's movements quickened. Soon our bodies were surging against one another's and it was a minor miracle that the Mount View Hotel's old walls didn't collapse outwards when we finally reached an explosion that should have been audible across the street.

For a long, long moment Victoria stayed poised above me, her back arched in exhausted enjoyment, before sliding slowly sideways until she lay beside me. I half-turned and kissed her gently. 'I had planned on this being a somewhat longer event,' I said.

'We have the rest of today, tonight, tomorrow and all the other days until . . . ' She broke off not wanting to add the final words. I knew why. I didn't want to think about the day, three weeks hence, when I would be climbing back onto a 747 at San Francisco airport.

'We'll worry about that later,' I told her.

'Some of the things we have to talk about can't be left too long.'

'I know.' She was right. If we were to make a life together the decision couldn't be left until I had one foot on the plane. It needed thought and planning, but for the moment I didn't feel like either. 'I'm hungry,' I said.

She laughed. 'My God, you haven't changed, have you?'

'In some things I have.' I had, too.

'Okay, we'll dress, have lunch, then, this afternoon we can . . . '

'I have plans for this afternoon,' I interrupted.

She turned towards me, her soft breasts pressing against my chest. 'So have I; fancy betting that they're the same?'

I shook my head. 'I don't bet on certainties.'

Easing away from me, Victoria climbed off the bed and raised the blind letting more sunlight into the room. We were at the back of the hotel and a few buildings were all that separated us from a marvellous view of the hills beyond the town.

'I hope Calistoga doesn't have a Peeping Tom,' I said as she stretched her arms high above her head, thrusting her naked breasts out against the window-pane.

I went into the bathroom, turned on the shower and let it run up to full temperature while I studied myself in the mirror. I looked tired, which wasn't really surprising, and I needed a shave. I had turned towards the door, planning to collect my shaving gear from my bag when glass shattered and simultaneously Victoria screamed.

I went into the bedroom fast and low,

absurdly aware of my nakedness. The window had crazed outwards from a hole about four feet above the floor.

Victoria was standing beside the window facing towards me, the palms of her hands pressed back against the wall. There was blood on her arms and across her breasts.

But it was the expression on her face that burned into me as I reached out to pull her down to the floor before dragging her into the bathroom. Her eyes were wide with the horror of someone waking from a nightmare and who has yet to realise that was all it was.

In the bathroom, I reached for my pants and struggled into them. From somewhere outside I could hear a voice shouting. It was a woman's voice and it sounded frightened.

Then Victoria spoke. 'My God,' she said softly, not to me but to herself. 'It's all happening again.'

3

When I was sure that Victoria's cuts were superficial I went out into the alley at the back of the hotel. By then I was sure I would find no-one but I was wrong.

The voice I had heard belonged to a thin-faced young girl who was one of a group of people ringing a small, freckly boy who looked ready for tears. He was no more than ten or eleven but the way the girl was talking he would be lucky to make twelve.

Smeeton, the desk clerk, was one of the crowd and he grabbed me by the arm, anxiously peering at me and clearly relieved to see that I was alive and well. 'You weren't hurt. Thank God for that.' The little boy looked even more relieved but tears were still close. Smeeton brandished an air-rifle at me. 'He used this.'

'He's always shooting off at things,' the

girl cut in. 'I told him he could kill someone.'

The clerk seized my arm again. 'Is your wife okay?'

I glanced at the small boy. There was nothing to be gained by making a big deal out of this. 'Shaken, but neither of us is hurt.'

Over the heads of the crowd I could see a burly uniformed figure coming towards us. Law and order was about to descend. 'Don't be too hard on him,' I said to no one in particular. I grinned at the boy. 'You didn't mean it, did you?'

The small boy looked up at me and shook his head. 'It wasn't me. Honest.'

The girl hit him. Tears started in earnest now. 'I didn't,' he insisted. 'I was shooting at that.' He pointed at a tree festooned with tin cans on strings. The tree was far enough away from the hotel to be safe from even the wildest shot.

The girl hit him again. Now I could see a facial resemblance and guessed they were brother and sister but it didn't mean she had to like him.

'I'll move you to another room,' the

27

desk clerk promised.

The uniform had arrived and I could see he was a Deputy Sheriff, maybe forty, with a moustache he could hide a bird in. I edged away from the group. The last thing I wanted was to start this holiday making statements to the local law.

'Honest, mister,' the boy said. 'I wasn't aiming this way.'

I smiled encouragement at him and went inside the hotel. This time, it took much longer for Victoria to unlock the door to room 37. She was fully dressed, and even in the haste of the moment she managed to look nothing short of sensational. She was wearing a medium length summer dress that mingled russet with beige; mixed browns were her best colours. She had tied her hair back with a strand of silk in beige streaked with reddish-brown. I was uncomfortably reminded of the splashes of blood on her body.

'Okay?' I asked.

She nodded.

'Do you need to see a doctor?'

'No. Just scratches.'

'It was some kid with an airgun,' I told her.

She nodded again.

I looked closely at her. There were white lines at the edge of her mouth and along the line of her nose. She was tight with suppressed tension. I put my arms around her and could feel trembling. 'Hey, come on, worse things happen every day on the streets of LA. Didn't you once tell me that guns are a way of life down there?'

I felt the nod of her head.

'Okay, then let's have lunch and you can show me Calistoga.'

The nod came again.

I kissed her lightly on the tip of her nose, then opened up my bag and raked out some creased but clean clothes to change into.

When I was shaved and dressed and held her in my arms again the trembling had stopped.

As we went down the stairs I told her my comment to the desk clerk and she agreed to play along. Neither of us wanted to start off by harassing a small boy into juvenile court.

Smeeton was talking on the telephone and covered the mouthpiece to tell us that the Deputy wanted us to call by later for a talk.

We took my car because Victoria told me that hers was down the street having a flat fixed.

She didn't much want to eat but I insisted and we drove out of town a few miles until we saw a place with tables on an open terrace. We sat under a stocky palm tree and studied one another in silence for a while. A blonde waitress, cheerful and capable, waved menus at us while rattling off a list of specials that she was sure we couldn't live without trying. We told her to bring whatever she thought best.

There were no other customers outside and only a couple of the inside tables were occupied.

'We must be fated,' I said. 'Everywhere we go people have a sudden urge to blast away with guns.'

'Don't joke about it.'

'Well, nothing's gained by taking it all

too seriously, is it?'

She nodded slowly and thoughtfully but I could see she didn't agree. She was simply avoiding an argument.

I rested a hand on her arm. 'I've missed you,' I told her.

For the first time since the window had shattered a full smile came onto her lips. 'I should hope you have.'

'You're supposed to tell me the same thing.'

She leaned across the table and kissed me softly on the lips. 'I've missed you.'

It needed willpower to continue making normal conversation. 'How's Teresa?' I asked, looking for a subject that would not raise my blood pressure. Teresa is Victoria's daughter from a marriage that went wrong. I have a daughter too, although I no longer have any serious responsibilities as my ex-wife remarried and can provide a stable home life with a man who is always home on time from the office, who is never called out in the middle of the night, only drinks too much at Christmastime and not because some nights that's the only way to get the dirt and squalor and blood out of his mind, and who doesn't brood over the fact that his work occasionally calls for him to shoot at people. And sometimes kill them. All things considered my daughter's stepfather is a much better deal than her real old man.

Victoria and her husband had both become cops and while that promoted understanding it had also led to days on end of no contact at all, exacerbated by her out-ranking him.

Both of us had had relationships since the ends of our respective marriages but, until last year in Los Angeles, there had been nothing that looked worth holding on to.

The blonde waitress arrived with a tray covered in enough food to feed a paddy-wagon full of cops and dexterously balanced it on one hand while she swept away a few white blossoms that had drifted onto the table from shrubs scattered between the palm trees. A light breeze kept the sun from feeling too hot and the decanter of white wine looked set to keep the temperature low.

'You'll like this,' the waitress commanded. 'It's our own.' She pointed down the hillside towards the rows and rows of carefully tended vines.

I poured some out for us and sipped mine. 'You're right,' I told the waitress.

'Sure I'm right, our vines have tender grapes.'

'MGM, 1945,' I said. 'Starring Edward G. Robinson and Margaret O'Brien.'

The waitress laughed. 'Don't forget the freckle-faced kid.'

'Jackie 'Butch' Jenkins.'

'Right!' The waitress laughed again. Embroidery on the pocket of her blue and white check coat told us her name was Sally. Maybe forty-five, she had the kind of face that could sell a million apple pies a year. 'You're English?'

'That's right.'

'But you know your movies.'

'Sign of a misspent youth.' That wasn't strictly true but I certainly had spent a lot of time in the local cinema near my Liverpool home. My mother had worked there and letting me in free was better than leaving me at home. My father couldn't look after me; his days were spent on the docks, his nights on various bandstands where he earned extra money playing not-bad alto saxophone in a dance band. The Beatles had hit such work on the head and very soon the bingo-callers had moved into the Astoria which put my mother out of work too. With their evenings free for the first time since their pre-marriage days my mother and father had discovered the penalties of having had to work day and night to keep us all in decent clothes and with food on the table; they didn't know one another any more.

'We sometimes have movie people in here,' Sally told us. 'They shoot *Harper's Valley* over in the next county.' I knew of it; a TV series in which everything and everyone was coated in solid varnish through which reality couldn't hope to gleam. Any talent there might be among crew and cast had a similarly hard time. Sally sighed. 'But they're not the same.'

It sounded as if she thought the same way as me, even if we were both guilty of feeling nostalgia for times which pre-dated our births. Suddenly all business, she cast a quick professional eye over our table to ensure we had all the right forks. 'Enjoy your lunch,' she instructed us before going back inside.

'You have another fan,' Victoria said.

'I make them everywhere I go.'

'Careful, I'm the jealous type.'

She wasn't and knew she didn't have to be. Reverting to my question, she told me about her daughter who at seventeen was already older than the age at which Victoria had borne her. Teresa was having boyfriend trouble; too many and, from Victoria's viewpoint, not enough discrimination. But Victoria didn't seem too worried; I gathered that she had brought up a pretty well-balanced child.

'It's beautiful here, isn't it?' she said.

The valley side rolled towards a river, which gleamed silvery far below us, then rolled back up again on the other side. The river ran almost due south which allowed grapes to grow abundantly on both slopes. Additionally, the hills were not too high, giving the sun a long day in which to toil in these particular vineyards.

Across the valley a pick-up whined along a steeply inclined dirt track between the rows of vines.

'What made you pick this place for us?' I asked.

Victoria didn't answer right away and I turned away from the view over the valley to look at her. A tiny crease was showing between her eyes. For a moment it crossed my mind that this region belonged to the past she had shared with her ex-husband or with another man, but as quickly as it came the thought went away. She would not have brought us to a place which carried such memories.

She saw me looking at her and a smile pushed aside the frown. 'I worked here one time. It was a case that caused a pile of problems for the local police. They decided it would help to have a couple of people working undercover so they sent to LA thinking 'Frisco and Sacramento were too close for security. Two of us came out.' The frown was back. 'Gerry Mandan and I had been working a vice detail together and were both due for transfer to homicide. Our Chief thought this would be a nice, easy way to run us in. A homicide out in the Napa Valley, four hundred miles from home and all the hassles of the big city. Only it didn't work out that way.'

'What happened?'

'For a while everything went well. Gerry and I homed in on a suspect and built a pretty good case for the Sheriff's office to act on. It wasn't necessary for us to go along for the arrest but we wanted to and no-one argued.' She paused, her food forgotten. After a moment she picked up her glass and sipped her wine but whatever the blonde waitress thought about its qualities, Victoria wasn't tasting it. All she was doing was moistening a mouth gone dry with an unwanted emotion.

After a moment she continued, her tone flat as if she was reciting some well-remembered facts from a dim archive of her mind. 'We were up in the hills beyond St Helena, that was where the suspect lived, and suddenly someone was shooting and the cops were shooting back and then Gerry and I were between them all. There was nothing we could do but join in. Gerry was hit. A bullet caught him in the throat. I shot the suspect. Five times. Any one of the shots would've killed him.' She set the wine glass down with a sharp, echoing click. From somewhere high overhead a bird screamed thinly. 'I was a hero for a day.' She smiled humourlessly. 'Back in LA I wasn't such a hero. Shooting a suspect five times isn't the way to win a citation down there. Here, well, maybe not here either but after what had happened in the valleys around St Helena and Calistoga I don't think anyone would've complained if I'd shot him a dozen times.'

'What did happen here?'

'Twelve homicides over a period of three years. For a while there was a theory that a serial killer was loose in the region but Gerry and I proved that wasn't so.' She reached out to rest a hand on mine. 'I'm sorry. Maybe we shouldn't have come here after all. It's just that I remembered this as a very beautiful place and one I've always wanted to return to. I really didn't think I would recall everything so clearly after all this time.'

'When did this happen?'

'Nearly ten years ago.' She made an effort at smiling. 'Too long to have memories, isn't it?'

I shook my head. 'Of course it isn't.' I had my own banks of unwanted memories and even if they didn't include pumping five bullets into a man they came close. Only the numbers were changed. 'Come along,' I said. 'Let's go back to town, talk to the Sheriff, and then we can make a start on this holiday.'

4

The Deputy Sheriff I had seen behind the
hotel was looming large over the tele-
printer in the office down the street from
the hotel. He had a scowl on his face that
would have frightened off a latter-day
Dillinger but it turned out to be a result
of nothing more serious than the fact that
he had mislaid his glasses.

We quickly settled that we didn't want
to push this and it was clear that neither
did he. The Deputy's name-tag told me
his name was J. D. Collis and despite his
bulk he turned out to be a deceptively
gentle character whose views on dealing
with children caught in acts like that of
the small boy with the airgun were closer
to those of a social worker than a cop. On
my patch such attitudes were luxuries I
didn't often enjoy but had I been him and
worked here I think I would have gone
along.

'Denny isn't a bad kid,' Collis told us.

'Just runs wild, like his sister, although she's probably the only one who keeps him in check.' He finally found his glasses, put them on and smiled at us both. When he looked at Victoria his eyebrows went up which is not an unusual response from any red-blooded male. 'Only thing is,' he went on, 'Denny doesn't usually lie.' He shrugged. 'I guess this time he was pretty badly frightened.'

'So we can forget it,' I said.

'I guess so. Staying long?'

'A while.'

'Your name's Mace and you're English,' Collis said.

'That's right.'

'What kind of business are you in, Mr Mace?'

I glanced at Victoria and shrugged. 'I'm a police officer.'

Collis said nothing, then looked at Victoria again. 'The clerk at the hotel said you were Mrs Mace.'

Victoria's skin darkened slightly and I grinned, mildly enjoying her embarrassment but only because I didn't expect it.

'My name is Bercovici,' she said.

Collis pursed his lips slightly and blew soundlessly. 'I was trying to figure how it was I knew you from someplace. You're a cop too.' He paused. 'Or you were, ten years ago.'

Victoria nodded slowly. One way or another, events were not allowing her to re-bury her memories.

'I was around at that time,' Collis continued. 'I was based in Santa Rosa then and wasn't too involved. But I remember all the excitement.' He grinned suddenly. 'You wouldn't remember me, I was about eighty pounds lighter then and I didn't have the disguise.' He touched his moustache with a forefinger. Then the smile faded. 'Of course, that maybe complicates things a little.'

'Why should it?' I asked.

He ignored me, his eyes still on Victoria. 'The kid with the airgun, Denny, and his sister Sharon, their name is Raskin.'

Victoria's colour changed again but this time it was to turn pale beneath her tan. She turned towards me, her dark eyes glowing with an expression I couldn't fathom but still did not like. 'That was his name,' she said. 'Raskin, Peter Raskin.'

'Whose name?' I asked, but was already guessing ahead.

'The man I . . . ' She broke off.

'The killer?'

She nodded.

I looked at Deputy Collis. 'Coincidence,' I said. 'That was ten years ago; that kid, Denny, he can't be more than ten or eleven now.'

'He's going on twelve.'

'Was Raskin their father?'

'Uncle.'

'Coincidence,' I said again.

'I guess you're right,' Collis said, although there was a touch of what could have been reluctance in this voice.

'Come on, Sheriff, the lieutenant only arrived in town last night. We know Denny couldn't have recognised her himself. Someone else would have had to do that, then tell Denny, then . . . ' I broke off, there was no point in continuing with this. Denny Raskin hadn't shot at Victoria deliberately; I knew it and Collis knew it. Victoria knew it too but she was still unhappy.

'You're right,' Collis said. 'Okay, let's all forget it and you folks have a nice stay here.'

'We shall,' I assured him. 'No statements?'

Collis shook his head. 'No, we'll do as I said and forget it.' He gestured over his shoulder. 'I'll hold onto the gun for a while though.'

Denny's airgun was lying on a table with a handful of pellets beside it. 'That might be for the best,' I agreed.

Outside we stood for a moment in the mid-afternoon heat. Victoria slipped a hand in mine and I squeezed it gently. 'Do you want to move on someplace else?' I asked.

'No, I'll be fine. It's just that I hadn't planned on all these memories. Just shows how dumb I really am. I should have known it would all come back, although I would never have guessed at it happening this way.'

'Let's go back to the hotel; I have ways of making you forget.'

She laughed for the first time since all

44

the unpleasantness began. 'You take the car to the hotel. I'll see you there in about ten minutes.'

'Where are you going?'

My sudden concern must have shown in my voice because she laughed again. 'Don't worry, I have to collect my car. The flat should be fixed by now.'

'Okay, but don't take long. I'm feeling impatient already.'

I watched her stride away, her movements simultaneously confident and sexy, her hair lifting and falling with each stride. I knew that, somehow, we had to work out a way to be together. Regardless of the bad start this visit to the Napa Valley had suffered, we had to end it in the right way.

I drove up to the hotel and parked beside the white camper which hadn't moved since my arrival. Instead of going inside I walked a short distance down the street, glancing in shop windows.

I was looking inside an unusually elegant bookshop when I heard a burst of excited laughter and turned to see a family which appeared to include about half a dozen kids and at least three dogs clambering into the white camper. I decided to leave the bookshop until another time and started back towards the hotel. A discreet bleep on a motor horn attracted my attention and Victoria waved as she drove past.

She was almost at the hotel when the white camper lurched backwards into the roadway. The braking lights on Victoria's car came on but she slid into the side of the camper with an echoing crunch.

I was running before any logical processes had begun; when they did they told me that the speed both vehicles had been travelling was so slow that the odds were no one was hurt.

I wasn't the first to reach the scene but while most people were clustering around the camper from which children and animals were streaming, I wrenched open the door of Victoria's Buick.

Her face was pale and her knuckles gleamed white where her hands gripped the steering wheel. Her head snapped around towards me. There was an angry glitter in her eyes which momentarily surprised me. Then she scrambled hurriedly from the car and together we went over to the driver of the camper.

He was shakingly apologetic. One of the dogs had taken it into its head to leap onto his lap as he started up and his foot had slipped causing the camper to jerk backwards without warning. He took full responsibility and, like the rest of the crowd, was more concerned over the kids than any damage to his vehicle.

It took a while to sort everyone out and discover that no one had been hurt and that the damage where Victoria's car had struck the camper would not prevent the family from continuing with their outing.

By the time all this was done and Victoria had parked her car with unexpected awkwardness and much stalling of the engine, I was beginning to think we would have had a quieter time had we taken our holiday in the middle of Los Angeles.

Inside the hotel the desk clerk, who had come out to see what all the fuss was about, told us he had moved our things into another, bigger, brighter room. I guessed that his motives were to keep us happy and unlikely to sue although the hassle with the other guest's camper was probably making him wish he could figure a way to send us along to the nearest rival hotel.

Our new room was at a corner and while it looked out over much the same view as before we had extra windows, a couch and a couple of comfortable arm chairs.

'That damned mechanic,' Victoria said as the door closed behind us.

'What mechanic?'

'All he had to do was fix a flat; and what happens? The brakes fail.'

'The brakes?'

'Why do you think I hit that camper? I'm not that bad a driver. I saw him coming out, knew he hadn't seen me and hit the brakes. They bit for a second, then went. That's why I couldn't park it easily, I had no brakes.'

I stood in the middle of the room, frowning at her. What was it I had said to Deputy Collis? The long arm of coincidence was rapidly shortening; another one and I would start having paranoid fantasies.

'Call the garage,' I said. 'Have them collect the car but I'll go along too.' I turned and opened the door.

'Where are you going?'

'I'll be back in a minute. Call the garage.'

I went down to the lobby and asked for the key to room 37. I told the clerk I couldn't find one of my credit cards. It wasn't the best of excuses but it served. Moments later I was in the room with the shattered window. It took longer than I expected to find what I was looking for because I wasted time searching at high level. It wasn't at high level, it was only about three feet above the floor and buried an inch or so into the side of a heavy oak wardrobe that stood against the wall opposite the window. I dug it out with a penknife that wasn't really designed for such tough work. I succeeded in making a mess of both the wardrobe and the blade.

The airgun Denny Raskin had been firing used small lead pellets like those that Deputy Collis had confiscated. This was small and lead but it wasn't an airgun pellet. It was a .22 calibre bullet.

I did my best to squint along a line from the hole in the wardrobe to the approximate point where the bullet had come through the window. One of the few buildings out back of the hotel was in direct line and near enough the right height if someone had stood on the rooftop.

Collis had been right when he'd said the small boy didn't usually lie; it wasn't he who had taken a shot at Victoria. It was someone else; and someone had recently made a bad job of repairing her car. A mistake which, if she hadn't had to brake suddenly while travelling slowly along Calistoga's main street, might well have resulted in something much messier than a damaged camper.

When the bullet came through the window Victoria had said something: It's all happening again. I had thought she meant the fact that the last time we were together bullets had flown. Now, adding together what had happened in the few short hours we had been in Calistoga and the story she had told me about her last visit here ten years ago, I knew she had meant something else.

It was those experiences which had led to the death of her colleague that were being repeated. I had an uncomfortable feeling, the kind all coppers get from time to time, that she was right.

5

The garage mechanic turned out to be guilty of nothing that an intensive course in personal hygiene couldn't straighten out. He had fixed the flat on Victoria's car within a half hour of her dropping the vehicle off last evening. Too busy to return it, he had parked the car out back and forgotten its existence until she called in. Anyone could have access to the parking lot and, hidden from the street as it was, anyone could have spent time working on the brakes. Undoubtedly, someone had done exactly that.

The job was neatly effective. Any sudden application of the brakes would have done the trick and if it had happened at high speed the results could have been decidedly messy. By nothing short of pure good luck Victoria had been obliged to hit the brakes while travelling at slow speed and apart from the crumpled front end of her Buick and the side panel of the tourist's camper no damage had been done.

We had to tell Deputy Collis, of course, because it was clear from the amount of sweat the garage mechanic was exuding that by the time the bars closed that night everyone in Calistoga would know about it. We persuaded Collis to bend the truth and also to lean on the mechanic to the same general effect; which was that a brake failure had occurred which resulted from an accident on the drive from LA. Collis wasn't too sure about any of it, especially knowing a gunman was loose in his town, but the fact that, even if neither Victoria nor I had any jurisdiction up here, we both outranked him convinced him to play it our way for the time being.

I told him we wanted to think about it all for a day or two, which was nothing less than the truth, because something very unpleasant seemed to be in the air.

'I'll give you forty-eight hours,' he said, confirming my suspicion that, given the chance, people talk just the way they do in the movies.

'Tell me what you did last evening,' I

said to Victoria when we left the Sheriff's office to walk back to the hotel.

'I checked in at around seven. Took the car down to the garage, walked back up Lincoln, ate at the diner over there.' She pointed across the street. 'Then I went back to the hotel and to bed.'

'What time was that?'

'A little after ten.'

'Did you go out this morning before I arrived?'

'No.'

'So, some time between seven last evening and ten, you were seen and recognised. Either that, or someone followed you from LA for reasons that have nothing to do with your last visit here.'

'I don't think so.'

Neither did I. 'You booked in here using my name,' I went on. 'So someone recognised you, not your name.'

'I used my name at the garage and the licence is in the car.'

It was a possibility but I didn't think so. Someone had seen Victoria and recognised her and decided to try to kill her. The use of the rifle showed he didn't care who knew it even if the coincidence of the kid playing with an airgun had confused matters for a while. Come to that, the job on the brakes also showed a marked lack of interest in concealing his intentions. If there had been a serious accident and if Victoria had been killed, even the most cursory inspection would have revealed tampering. Someone wanted Victoria either dead, or frightened off, and he didn't care who knew it.

We reached the hotel and went inside, heading for the bar by mutual and unspoken consent.

We soon concluded that we had nothing on which to mount an investigation whose roots were almost ten years old. We also came to the conclusion, very reluctantly, that we had no choice but to investigate. Having tried twice, however unsuccessfully, our man would have another crack and we couldn't take the risk of sitting around and doing nothing. Of course we could have left town and we considered that for a full thirty seconds before discarding the idea.

'For one thing, who's to say this guy won't follow us and try again some other place?' Victoria said.

'And, anyway, we're too conscientious at our work to walk away from a case,' I added.

Victoria raised an eyebrow over the rim of her glass and I grinned in acknowledgement that I wasn't being too serious in that remark. But it was, in part, true. Neither one of us would have been able to relax knowing that someone wanted Victoria dead or injured.

We finished our drinks. 'Another?' I asked. 'It's too early to eat.'

Victoria shook her head. 'Right now, what I want is to get laid.'

'You have such an elegant way with words,' I told her, but I wasn't arguing.

Neither of us was much in the mood for a long reflective bout of lovemaking. Maybe it was the two brushes with death, but there was an urgency to our actions and our movements that grew out of something more than the simple sexual excitement we took in one another's bodies.

Afterwards, lying close together, arms and legs entwined, a couple of thoughts drifted into my mind that had no business being there in the circumstances.

'Was Peter Raskin married?' I asked.

She frowned and I manoeuvred a finger to where I could smooth the crease away. 'Yes, he was. Why?'

'I've been busy assuming the shot and the brakes were the work of a man. It could be a woman. Especially seeing the rifle was small calibre.'

Victoria eased herself partly upright, propping her head against one hand. Her warm breasts pressed against my chest. It was a very comfortable feeling and didn't sit at all well with the conversation we were having. 'Her name was Karen. She was small, dark-haired, quite pretty but always angry-looking.'

'How did she take it when her husband was accused of the killings?'

'She didn't believe it, but, then, how many women would believe their husband was a multiple murderer?'

'Did you see her after he died?'

Victoria shook her head, hair falling across her face.

I tried out the other thought. 'You're, what, thirty-three now? So you were around twenty-four when you were here last.'

'Yes. In fact I had a birthday while we were up here.' A shadow passed over her face. 'Gerry Mandan and I went out for dinner to celebrate. He made a pass at me that night. The only time he ever did. I turned him down and he didn't push it. He was a very nice guy. That was a week before Peter Raskin shot him.'

'What did you look like when you were twenty-four?'

She frowned questioningly. 'Pretty much the same as I do now.'

'How about hairstyle? That can make quite a difference.'

'For God's sake, Mace, I can't remember how I wore my hair all that time ago.'

'Of course you can, unless you changed it every week and I don't think the LAPD will have allowed you enough time for that.'

'Why are you interested?'

'If we're ruling out someone from LA, then the gunman had only a passing glimpse of you last night. That means your face was burned on his mind. For that to happen he must have had both cause and opportunity. Cause would be if he was close to Peter Raskin; opportunity would be if he had seen a lot of you last time you were here. Or she, if it's a woman. Raskin's wife would have cause, how about opportunity? Did you spend much time with her?'

Victoria thought for a moment. 'I interviewed her once for maybe twenty minutes and she was present the first time I interviewed her husband.'

'So she would have fair chance of committing your face to memory.'

'I suppose so.'

'So, what about that hairstyle?'

'Similar, maybe shorter and with more curl in it.'

'What was all that about not being able to remember?'

'There's a reason, so stop being smug.'

'What reason?'

'Karen Raskin wore her hair the same way. I can see her clearly in my mind.'

'And maybe she can see you just as clearly. I think we should go talk to her.' I slid away from her and started up from the bed but she pulled me back.

'Not now,' she said.

'Why not? Can you think of something better to do?'

Her hands and her mouth made several suggestions and I quickly forgot Karen Raskin but then the telephone rang and spoiled what had all the makings of a highly entertaining evening. I would have let it ring but Victoria reached for it with the instinct of someone for whom the telephone acts like a starting-gun. She spoke, then listened, then told whoever it was that we would both be delighted. After she had returned the phone to its rest she told me what we would both be delighted to do this evening.

'The man with the camper, his name is Greg Lewis, he wants to buy us a drink to apologise for causing the accident.'

'I don't want to spend the evening with half a dozen kids and God knows how many dogs; and, anyway, it wasn't all his fault.'

'He doesn't know about the brakes, and he never will, and the kids and the dogs stay behind. The hotel is providing a baby-minder on the house. It's just Lewis and his wife.'

'Damn it, Victoria . . . ' But she wasn't listening to my objections.

'There's some kind of function at one of the county's leading wineries. There'll be a crowd of local people and we could do worse than mingle. We might pick up something on Raskin and his family.'

She was in the bathroom by the time she was finished speaking and even if I'd chosen to argue she wouldn't have heard over the sound of the shower. So I gave up, without too much grace, joined her in the shower and very quickly lost any feeling of irritation. Not that the shower is the best place to do what we did; but concentrating on staying upright at least took my mind off other things.

6

The function turned out to be a huge publicity bash designed to draw to the attention of the great wide wine-buying world the fact that Sam Monahan's Laronne Winery was about to launch a new range. I hadn't seen so many people clutching wine glasses in one gathering since my days as a young copper assigned to keep an eye on the wedding of one of Liverpool's richest pools promoters. Here, however, about ten miles west of Calistoga at the end of a mile-long driveway, the setting was considerably better.

The drive helped set up the house. One side of the smooth blacktop surface was lined with lemon trees interspersed with dark-leaved cedars whose branches spread low over the car. A double-decker bus wouldn't have made it but, then, I don't suppose there are many in America, least of all likely to call on the owner of

Laronne. The other side of the drive was marked by short metal posts between which hung chains, all painted white making it easy for drivers who didn't like to use their brains to find the road. Beyond the chains was a rolling expanse of immaculate grass. If there were any daisies or other interlopers brave enough to show their faces on the lawn, I couldn't see them from the car. In any event, there was probably a team of gardeners lurking behind the trees ready to leap out if anything other than a blade of grass risked poking its head above the soil.

The house was built of dark-red brick and followed a design that was a cross between Ruritanian and early Walt Disney. Floodlights nestled amongst dark-green ivy. The air was heavily scented. It could have been natural but I didn't think so. Nature was neither good enough nor sufficiently reliable. Money had been spent lavishly to make this function a success; even the gravel on the paths looked as if it had been shampooed for the occasion. If someone could have figured a way to polish up the stars and dust off the moon they surely would have done so.

The building was topped off by a spectacular, curving expanse of gleaming red pantiles lit from floodlights suspended amidst an array of assorted domes and spires. Peeping through the ivy-clad walls more lights hung from phoney leaded windows. Any moment I expected Janet Leigh to open one and throw down a knotted sheet.

Inside, the house followed the design of those old Bette Davis movies that were supposed to be set in England. Lots of hand-cut stone, armorial shields, crossed swords, stags' heads, and floors of polished hardwood. It was surprisingly attractive even if England was never like this. The furniture was solid and expensive; brass and copper whatsits covered most surfaces and everything glowed comfortably in the light from crackling log fires. They were definitely only for appearance as the night was hot.

Our companions for the evening were not as bad as I'd feared. Greg Lewis was a college professor from somewhere in

Idaho, the name of which I didn't quite catch, and he supplemented his income by writing a newspaper column on wine. His invitation to this launch had encouraged the Lewises to take their annual vacation in California even if it had meant sneaking away before the semester finished. He taught classical languages and I gathered there wasn't much call for such things in Idaho. He was a slightly nervous character with blond hair worn in a crewcut that had been out of fashion since before he was born. His wife, Linda Lee, was a calm, placid and extremely pregnant young woman. This was to be her fourth child. The extra kids I had seen piling into and out of the camper were just along for the vacation.

Lewis seemed to know a lot of people and he insisted on introducing us but the names soon sounded alike and the people behind the names certainly looked alike. The men were mostly young, marginally overweight, deeply tanned, and aggressively outgoing in their pastel-coloured linen suits. The women were mostly younger, large-breasted and mildly predatory, wearing original dresses which displayed as much as possible of their even deeper tans. Everyone was talking too loud, drinking too fast, and appeared to have too many very white teeth. I had the impression that I was watching some kind of contest the rules of which were known only to the players. It was clear we could expect no information from these people except maybe the addresses of their dentists and dressmakers. I wanted to take Victoria back to Calistoga but we had made the grave logistical error of bringing the Lewises with us in my car; now we were stuck until they decided to return to the hotel. From the way Lewis was sampling the non-vintage, that was unlikely to be much before dawn.

When Linda Lee struck up a conversation with another young woman in an almost equally advanced state of pregnancy I pulled Victoria away from the throng and we went outside where the air was warm, the stars were bright, and I was strongly inclined towards sex in the shrubbery. Victoria wasn't playing, however.

'I gave up that kind of thing the year I became pregnant,' she told me.

'I don't think I want to hear any more about that.'

'Neither do I, so cool off, Mace, until we're back in the hotel.'

'When will that be? Lewis is set for the night.'

She kissed me on the lips which, given the state I was in, was not a kind thing to do. 'Patience.'

'Hello there,' a familiar voice said.

It was Sally, the waitress from the place where we had eaten lunch. With her was a thin, wiry individual with near-white hair that looked out of place as his face was youthfully unlined. Sally introduced us. His name was Andy Morgan and they were married. It turned out they owned the restaurant where we had lunched but their own smalltime efforts at winemaking were not seen as serious competition to the owner of Laronne.

'If we were, old Sam would never have invited us here,' Sally said. 'He hates competition, thinks he has a God-given right to produce wine and anyone else trying it in the Napa Valley is an enemy.'

'He must have a lot of enemies,' Victoria said.

'They're getting fewer, he's outliving 'em.'

'Sally,' her husband said, his tone mildly warning.

'I'm entitled, I was a member of the family for a time.'

'Oh?'

'I married Cliff Monahan when he was young and crazy and I was old enough to know better.'

'Who's he?'

Sally looked at me curiously. 'Cliff is Sam's son. Sam Monahan owns this place, and about one-third of the property in St Helena too. How come you're invited here if you don't know that?'

I explained about the wine-writing college professor.

'Come along,' Sally said. 'I'll introduce you to old Sam. If you don't meet him your education won't be complete.'

Without giving me a chance to argue she led me back into the big house with her husband and Victoria trailing behind. I could hear Andy Morgan's mild protests but Sally ignored them. I didn't care too much one way or the other; as we couldn't leave and the shrubbery was off limits, we had to pass the time somehow.

Sam Monahan was a short, stocky man with a hooked nose and grey-streaked hair. He looked like a compressed Broderick Crawford, his barrel chest straining against the confines of a midnight-blue silk suit.

When he heard my accent he launched into a tirade against the European Economic Community, its wine lake, unfair taxation, tariffs and a whole string of complaints none of which I understood. I interrupted to tell him that I was a harmless holidaymaker with no more knowledge of the wine industry than could be gleaned from a passing acquaintance with the English licensing laws.

Monahan glared at me for a moment, then demanded to know what the hell I was doing at his house. There was more aggression than seemed necessary.

'At the moment I'm wishing I could find a way to get out of here. If you're thinking of throwing me out I would take it as a gesture of everlasting friendship.'

He looked at me closely, as if weighing his chances. We both knew they were slim and after a moment he managed a thin smile. 'Sorry. I thought you might be one of those bastards who . . . ' He stopped, took a deep breath, swelling his chest against the blue silk suit. There was a sheen of perspiration on his top lip. He had a problem but he had decided that it had nothing to do with me.

'I may be a bastard and a gatecrasher, but I'm harmless,' I assured him.

He nodded slowly, the smile widening a little. 'What line are you in?' he asked.

I hesitated, not wanting to tell him but at the same time aware that there was no point in lying. So I told him. Almost at once Monahan's attitude changed to one of bear-hugging friendliness.

Soon, Victoria had to reveal that she too was a police officer and Monahan almost burst his buttons. He was a police-freak. I've met members of the clan before. Usually, they are far-right members of the hang 'em or flog 'em brigade with an attitude towards law-breakers that makes even the toughest coppers seem like limp-wristed liberals. Monahan insisted that we should look at his gun collection and we were dragged away from Sally and Andy Morgan.

Monahan's study was high ceilinged with mahogany-panelled walls. The kind of room which most men would fill with books or sporting trophies or booze or whatever else occupied their idle hours. Sam Monahan had filled it with enough fire-power to start, or even finish, a small war. Some were real collectors' items: a pair of Navy Colts, once used by a member of the James gang; a sub-machine gun, used in the Arcadia ambush that ended the careers of Bonnie and Clyde; a silver-plated Derringer, once worn strapped to the thigh of a girlfriend of Al Capone. I didn't argue with Monahan, despite grave doubts about the accuracy of his claims. He was not the kind of man to argue with, especially not here in a room which held more than two hundred firearms.

The old-style weapons with histories attached were in a distinct minority. Most of the guns were modern, in full working order, and none was locked away. They were all loaded too, which served only to increase my feeling of disquiet.

Victoria didn't seem too worried about it all. Maybe her day-to-day experience of firearms had hardened her even to displays like this.

Monahan eagerly recounted the fire-power of individual weapons, displaying even more enthusiasm than he had in his attack on the iniquities of the EEC's policy towards wine exporting to the United States.

'What do you use?' he suddenly demanded, addressing Victoria.

'A Smith and Wesson .32.'

'You have it with you?'

To my surprise, Victoria nodded and opened a handbag she had held all evening. Despite my momentary qualm when she had pressed a cold metal key against my neck at the hotel I had not given any thought to the fact that she would have a gun with her. Even after the events earlier in the day it had not occurred to me to ask if she was armed. It was a slightly disconcerting feeling, that she had brought a gun with her to our reunion. It was unjustified, I know; carrying a gun was probably second nature, but it didn't stop me feeling uneasy.

She showed Monahan the gun. He took it from her, handling it expertly.

'Five-shot?'

'It's less bulky than the six-shot.'

He nodded approvingly. 'Useful weapon.' He eyed her with sudden curiosity. 'You ever killed a man?'

Victoria stared at him for a moment, then took the gun and put it back in her bag. She turned towards me, then, as if realising there was nothing to be gained by walking out, she nodded her head. 'It goes with the job.'

'Well, I'll be damned.' Monahan looked at me. 'You too?'

'Yes.'

'Jesus.' His eyes held an admiring

gleam. I can do without that kind of admiration. Then his expression changed, becoming thoughtfully conspiratorial. 'You say you're here on vacation?'

'That's right.'

'You here on business?' he asked Victoria.

She assured him she wasn't.

'Listen, there's something you can maybe help me with.' His voice had changed along with his expression. The heartiness had gone and he sounded almost like a child about to ask for something he knows will be refused.

Then, before he could continue, a woman's voice came from the open doorway. 'Ah, there you are, Sam. You know you're neglecting your guests and one or two of them are growing fractious.'

She was slender, quite small, middle-aged and was smiling politely at Victoria and me, thus offsetting the implied rebuke at our gatecrasher status. She was thin-faced and her hair, greying-blonde, showed little signs of the endless care and attention most of the other women here had showered on themselves.

'Okay, Ruth,' Monahan said. 'This is Ruth Beckerman,' he added. 'She helps out with these fests. Need a woman's touch and . . . Ruth provides it.' He grasped my arm in his right hand and Victoria's in his left. 'They're police officers,' he told the woman. 'He's English and she's American. What were those names again?'

'Mace,' I said. 'And this is Victoria.' I deliberately left out Victoria's second name. The fewer people who knew, the fewer would associate her with past events. Until we found out who was trying to kill her, that seemed like a good idea.

'And you've been talking about guns, haven't you.' Ruth shook her head. 'What have I told you?'

Monahan boomed an echoing laugh that sounded more than a mite forced and stepped forward to bear-hug the woman. She let him do it with a tolerant smile on her face. 'Ruth's a psychiatrist,' he told us. 'Has a whole string of long words to tell you what my gun collection means. Don't believe one goddamn word of it.' He laughed again and strode off down the corridor with an arm still wrapped tightly around Ruth Beckerman. 'See you later,' he yelled back over his shoulder.

'Not if I can help it,' I said quietly.

A man's voice came from directly behind us. 'Sounds like treason. Don't you know such attitudes are not encouraged here in the kingdom of Laronne?'

He was tall and lean with dark curling hair and pleasant light-brown eyes. Although tanned and with the usual whiter-than-white teeth, he didn't have the clone-like appearance of most of the other men I had seen earlier. For one thing he had a crooked nose that was decidedly non-regulation issue.

'I'm shell-shocked,' I said.

He grinned. 'I know the feeling.'

'You've seen the gun collection?' Victoria asked.

'Seen it? You really are strangers, aren't you. I grew up with it. I'm Cliff Monahan, Sam's my father.' The grin widened. 'Try not to hold that against me. If it helps, I'm terrified of guns.'

'It helps,' Victoria said.

'Ruth keeps trying, but he'll never part with the collection.'

'She wants him to?'

Cliff Monahan's smile faded. 'Everyone does. Laraine did too, before . . . ' His voice trailed off and there was a moment of silence before, suddenly, the smile was back. 'Come along, I'll buy you a drink to wash away the taste of cordite.' He opened a door. 'We'll go this way. I have to find what's happened to the band.' He glanced at Victoria, then at me, then back again. 'There'll be dancing later, for those who can still keep their feet.'

'I haven't danced in years,' she told him.

I hadn't either and even then I'd been clumsy and about as useful as a third Nicholas brother. 'Don't expect much help from me,' I said.

Cliff Monahan's smile widened. 'Do I see an opening? One of the advantages of my previous career was that I learned every step ever invented.'

'What career was that?'

'I ran a night club in San Francisco;

best place in town for dancing.' He laughed quietly. 'At least that's what our advertising claimed.'

We had negotiated our way along a passage high and wide enough to take one of those double-decker buses that never came here, and our guide opened another door. This one led into the kitchens. Five dinner-jacketed men were crowded in one corner, laughing and drinking.

'Jesus,' Cliff said. 'Musicians!' But he didn't sound mad about it, just resigned. Most of them were youngsters although one, a man I recognised from pictures on record sleeves, was a little older. A bass-player of considerable merit, Monty Budwig was the leader of the group but most musicians, especially young ones, have minds of their own. Here, the food and drink, to say nothing of the predatory women in their body-revealing dresses, were proving more interesting than making music. Monty and Cliff did what they could to hustle the band out of their corner and onto a stage set up in the main hall. While the rest of the band set up, Monty and I talked about mutual friends and acquaintances. Among these was Bill Berry with whom Monty sometimes worked in LA. Bill had helped me out during the fracas Victoria and I were involved in during my last visit to California.

With the band finally launched, however reluctantly, into their first number, Victoria persuaded me to dance. I didn't argue although as far as I was concerned it was little more than walking the beat to music.

'What do you suppose Sam Monahan wanted?' Victoria asked.

I was too busy concentrating on not stepping on her feet to give the question much thought. 'He probably wants a rival rubbing out.'

'I think he's a worried man.'

'It isn't our problem,' I told her. I risked a glance around me. The hall which had become a ballroom for the evening was high enough for clouds to form. William Randolph Hearst would have loved it. He could have kept Marion's pet poodle in it. I stepped on a moving object and started to apologise to

Victoria but all I'd done was dance on my other left foot.

I think we were both relieved when Cliff Monahan cut in. I took the opportunity to go in search of the Lewises. By now the wine stocks of the Laronne winery had been drastically diminished and there was a greater concentration of drunks this side of Glasgow on Hogmanay although so far none of them had started fighting. I saw no sign of either Greg or Linda Lee and spread my net a little wider.

Along one side of the house was a covered walkway paved in pink stones and liberally scattered with tubs of flowers. I went down the arbour, carefully picking my way among several copulating couples and a fair number of semi-conscious imbibers. Given Linda Lee's state of pregnancy she would not have been among the former but I checked just in case Greg was there, or I could learn some new technique. He wasn't and I didn't.

Quite suddenly I found myself eavesdropping on Sam Monahan. His voice was coming from inside the house and he was obviously talking into a telephone.

'For Christ's sake, you can't keep on doing this,' he was saying.

Any instinct I might have had to politely creep away faded at his next words.

'Someone will get killed.'

I waited.

'No, no, I don't mean that.' He was hoarsely ingratiating.

Another pause.

'Okay, okay. Tomorrow.'

I heard the telephone slam down on its cradle with considerable force.

'The bastards,' Sam Monahan said. The epithet was spoken softly, without aggression, but it carried a wealth of menace. The owner of Laronne was very angry and, as Victoria had suggested, he was certainly a worried man.

After a moment I heard a door open and close and I took the opportunity to move away from the window and go in search of my companions. Monahan's problems really were none of my business. I had enough to worry over

81

without any further hassles, but I had to make an effort to quell natural, if not professional, curiosity.

A woman's voice, calling my name, took me away from snooping. It was Linda Lee Lewis and she had her husband with her. At least Greg was present in body if not in any other respect. I didn't know what he would say in his column for the newspaper back home but he would surely be an expert on hangovers by the morning.

I carried Greg to where I had left the car, dumped him against the front wheel and went in search of Victoria while Linda Lee hovered over her husband trailing a stream of apologies after me. It wasn't necessary, I was happy at the chance to leave.

Victoria was still with Cliff Monahan although they were no longer dancing. Instead they were talking with a startlingly beautiful young woman with short blonde hair, skin like satin, a megawatt smile and a body which almost refused to stay inside a brilliant red silk dress. Not many women can wear red bright enough to find in the dark without looking like a low-class hooker. This girl was an exception.

She was Cliff's wife, but she didn't look married and there was a wayward gleam in her eyes that suggested keeping her in line would be a full-time occupation.

She was telling Victoria that she was an actress and had just landed a part in *Harper's Valley*, the soap which was filmed largely in San Francisco and at locations in the Napa Valley.

'Next year at this time, the name Holly Monahan will mean money in the bank,' she said, laughing with delight at the prospect.

I hadn't assumed the Monahans to be short of the necessary green stuff but maybe Cliff was too tight for Holly's comfort. Or maybe she just wanted to be independent. Or just wanted more.

She had an openly cheerful attitude towards her ambitions. I liked her and wanted to talk but I couldn't let Linda Lee stay where she was. Reluctantly, I told Victoria that we should go and why.

Cliff Monahan said he would call us

and arrange to meet. I glanced at Holly and the gleam in her eye appeared even more wayward than before.

'Jesus, Mace, why didn't you lay her right there,' Victoria said as we walked back to the car.

'Jealous?'

She dug me in the ribs by way of an answer so I stopped and held her close to me. 'Listen to me, we have a lot to settle while I'm here and we're being side-tracked enough as it is. Don't raise trouble where none exists.'

'I saw how you were looking at one another.'

'She's an attractive woman.'

'And as obvious as . . . '

I cut off her remarks with a kiss. 'Cut it out,' I said.

'Don't try being masterful,' she told me. 'It won't work.'

I grinned at her and she laughed and when we kissed again it was as warm as ever.

Back at the car we decided that the best place for Greg Lewis was the front passenger seat where he could be strapped more or less upright. I favoured strapping him to the roof but didn't say so as Linda Lee was showing signs of overtiredness.

I started up the motor, found some early-morning headache-easing music on the radio, and moved off down the long driveway. In my headlights the trees looked ghostly and the white fence posts and chain allowed me to put my brain in neutral.

I was taking a long right-hand curve when there was a thud from the front of the car as a tyre burst. The affected wheel dug in and the angled momentum of the car sent the wheel spinning out of my hands. If I had been driving slowly that would have been all there was to it, but the combination of a very long and eventful day and the temptation of a traffic-free driveway had nudged the speed up just a little too much.

The car began to roll over into the fencing and at the same moment Linda Lee screamed loud enough to penetrate even her husband's drink-sodden brain. Greg came awake and began yelling;

Victoria, who was sitting directly behind him spoke but I couldn't make out the words and, anyway, I was too busy trying to regain control of the car.

I didn't succeed and the car rocked over onto its side and there was a screech of metal on metal and then a shrill clatter of breaking glass.

Another scream came from behind me but I couldn't tell whether it was Linda Lee or Victoria. Then, with a sickening suddenness, the scream was cut off as one of the metal fencing posts slid through the shattered window and into the rear compartment.

Greg Lewis was on top of me, struggling against the restraint of the seat belt. Somehow, he snapped it loose and one flailing arm hit me glancingly on the jaw.

Half-dazed, I turned to look behind me. Both women were lying crumpled and silent up against the off-side door of the car which was now resting on the ground. A glimmer of moonlight came in through the windows which faced upwards. It wasn't much but it was enough to show me the spreading dark stain that could only be blood on them both.

Then, Greg Lewis's foot came at me out of the gloom and, wedged in as I was, I couldn't avoid it. This time he struck me square on the side of the head, just in front of the ear.

I passed out.

7

I knew I had not been out for more than a few seconds because Greg Lewis's legs were still threshing dangerously. On the radio Fats Waller was playing 'Rosetta', his celeste tinkling delicately against the engine's roar as the road wheels spun freely at high speed.

I turned off the ignition and pushed myself upright. Lewis, feeling my movement, began asking what had happened; his voice was slurred, but he was clearly a sight less drunk than he had been a few minutes before.

A soft-voiced moan came from the rear compartment and then I heard my name spoken.

'Okay, take it easy,' I told Victoria. 'I'll have you out of there in a second.'

I was too optimistic. Long, dragging minutes passed before I had heaved Lewis up and out. I left him sprawled on the grass to scramble back onto the car.

Pulling open the rear door I leaned in to Victoria and Linda Lee. As I did so Victoria looked up at me. Moonlight touched her face, turning it ghostly pale.

'Oh, Christ, Mace,' she said softly. 'She's dead.'

I slid down inside and checked; I didn't disbelieve her, I simply didn't want to accept that she was right.

The metal fencing post that had come through the window and passed by me had struck Linda Lee squarely in the chest.

'What about the baby?'

Victoria moved and in the faint light from the brightly moonlit night sky I could see she was placing her head on Linda Lee's abdomen.

'I can't hear anything,' she said. 'We need a doctor and an ambulance and we need them fast.'

I scrambled from the car and between us we heaved the heavy body up and out, not caring now for the mother but hoping against hope that her child would survive. When she was stretched out on the grass by the side of the driveway I checked

Greg. He was sleeping. In the circumstances it was the best thing that he could
do. The immediate future was unlikely to
hold many restful moments for him.

I had started back towards the house
when headlights from a vehicle coming
up the driveway from the direction of the
road flickered across the trees. Moments
later it seemed that whatever gods
watched over the Lewis family were
paying attention once more. The driver
was Deputy Collis and there was no need
for valuable wasted moments being spent
in explanations.

Victoria went with Collis, Linda Lee
and the still-dazed Greg to the hospital. I
borrowed a heavy-duty flashlamp from
Collis and left it blinking its warning
message as I headed for the house.

I found a pair of Laronne employees,
solid-looking individuals whose duties
included staying sober, and they took me
back to the wreck in a four-wheel drive
two-truck. To clear the road we hauled
the rental car further through the gap
smashed in the fencing, in the process
dropping it back on all fours.

I refused a lift back to the house, saying I would walk up later. The two men glanced at one another but they earned their living obeying orders and didn't argue. As their tow-truck disappeared towards the house I used the Deputy's flashlamp to check over the car.

By now I had abandoned forever any thoughts about ill-luck, coincidence or any of those other things that explain away the inexplicable. Flat tyres come in all kinds and only rarely cause a smash as bad as this.

Almost all the tyre and a sizable chunk of wheel were missing. I sniffed at the wheel. It wasn't very scientific but I would have bet my boots on a small explosive charge having done the deed.

Now there was no doubt that someone wanted to do more than frighten or warn Victoria. This was the work of a man prepared to kill and who didn't care who suffered. Whatever he might or might not have been before, he was now a murderer.

I heard a sound and turned to see a vehicle coming down from the house.

It was the tow-truck with one of the

heavies at the wheel; sitting beside him was Sam Monahan.

'Jesus Christ, Mace, what happened?'

'A blow-out,' I said.

'Were you alone? What happened to . . .'

'They're on their way to the hospital with Sheriff Collis.'

'Anyone badly hurt?'

I nodded.

'How bad?'

'Linda Lee Lewis is dead.'

He didn't know her and I didn't feel like explaining.

Monahan reached into the tow-truck, switched on a powerful searchlight and sprayed the beam over the wrecked car. 'Haul it up to the house, Eddie,' he said. The heavy grunted. 'And have the fence fixed.' He shone the light down to the ground where the grass was all gouged up. 'Call the gardener and have him come down here right away. He'll need turf.'

I couldn't believe this. After what had happened all he wanted was to erase every sign of the incident.

'For Christ's sake, Monahan . . .'

'I run a business here. Those people up at the house are customers, buyers. I don't want them frightened off booze.'

I wanted to tell him to leave it where it was, that the local forensic team would want to go over the car and the scene but it wouldn't have done any good. Sam Monahan was not a man accustomed to taking orders, and cop-freak or no cop-freak, he had a sense of priorities. Something in his tone told me that law and order and its day-to-day requirements were not high priority.

I let it go. The most important thing about the explosive could be determined whether the car was here on the lawn or at the Calistoga police pound or up at Sam Monahan's house.

At the house Monahan insisted on lending me a car. The way he said it I gathered there were enough around the place to keep me going in case car-wrecking became endemic, the way it had on my last visit to California. I hoped death would not become similarly frequent.

An uneasy thought flickered across my

mind. Until I knew better, everyone was suspect but I had let Victoria go off with Deputy Collis. I asked Monahan why Collis might have been over this way.

'I had to call him about . . . I asked him over for a drink.'

I hadn't missed the hesitation. 'Why did you really call him? To check up on me?'

He nodded slowly, his eyes hooded. 'Your friend too. She's Lieutenant Bercovici. Tough lady.'

'Collis has a loose mouth.'

'He's a good cop,' Monahan insisted. 'He keeps the county clean.'

'Do you pay him?'

'Hell, no. He's straight.'

I guessed he was probably speaking the truth. Collis hadn't seemed the type to take money, even if he was unexpectedly talkative.

We reached a garage big enough to house several cars and a couple of trucks. Down at the far end Eddie was unhitching the wrecked rental car.

'What do you want doing with it?' Monahan asked.

'Nothing. Collis will need to take a look, forensic too.'

'Forensic?'

'There might be a problem.'

Monahan took hold of my arm, his fingers gripping tightly. 'What the hell happened out there?'

'The problem isn't yours.'

'How can you know that?'

I suppose I couldn't, not for sure, and the curiosity I'd felt at hearing his earlier telephone conversation bubbled back. I knew I could be wrong about what had happened to the car. I didn't think I was, but I had to admit a possibility that this time it hadn't been an attempt on Victoria's life, even if the only person I admitted it to was me. 'I'm sure,' I told Monahan.

For a moment he thought about arguing, then changed his mind. 'Speaking of problems, I have my share.'

'So I gathered, but this has nothing to do with you.'

He looked up at me, his head tilted like a hawk eyeing possible breakfast. 'No?'

I shook my head firmly.

'I thought someone had made a mistake and . . . ' His voice trailed off.

'And done what, Mr Monahan?'

'Call me Sam,' he said, pulling a smile from somewhere before releasing my arm.

'Earlier you were about to ask for help, Sam.'

He stared up at me. 'From what you're saying, or not saying, you have enough trouble.'

'We have, but if you want to tell me about yours, I'll listen.'

He was thinking hard. He had seemed eager to seek help when we were in his gun-room; now he wasn't. Maybe it was the telephone conversation I'd overheard, maybe it was what had happened to my car. Then he leaned back against a work-bench and sighed. 'Okay, I'll tell you, but I have to admit I'm not sure I want you to take risks for me on top of everything else.'

I realised he meant what he was saying. I had misjudged the little man. He wasn't the completely hard-nosed character I'd thought him to be. It also occurred to me that regardless of any problems Sam

Monahan might have, quite clearly he had influence in some quarters. His backing could help me when I asked the questions that needed answering. 'Tell me about it,' I said.

He smiled, obviously relieved at the chance to talk. 'For the past six months our trucks have been hit regularly. Sometimes the hijackers dump the load, other times they pour chemicals into the tankers. Twice a driver was forced off the road and the truck wrecked. Then we've had plant breakdowns, bad ones that screw up a complete batch.'

'A rival?'

'I don't think so. Sure we have competition but there's never been anything like this before and there's no cause for it now. Why, some of the people here and in Somona County have been making wine for three generations.'

'Who then?'

'All I know is some guy keeps calling me and telling me he has a solution to my problem, but he won't tell me what it is.'

'Is he the one who called tonight?'

Monahan straightened up, his expression hardening.

'I was outside the window, looking for Greg Lewis. I overheard your end of the conversation.'

He stared at me for a moment before deciding I was speaking the truth. 'That's right. And this time, he said he was ready to lay it all on the line. He's coming here tomorrow with a deal.'

'What kind of deal?'

'He didn't say, but it's pretty damn clear he's planning to make me an offer I can't refuse.' He managed a weak smile.

'And you want me to be here when he comes?'

'No, he told me no one should be around or there'll be big trouble. He's threatening this time to send in helicopters and spray this section of the valley with defoliant.'

I had an uneasy feeling I was getting out of my depth. Liverpool can be a rough town, standing as it does on the most direct route into England from Ireland, but this was something else. 'You believe that?' I asked.

He nodded soberly. 'These guys are connected.'

'Connected?'

'The Organisation.'

'The Mafia?'

I must have sounded incredulous because he took care with his answer. 'That's a name I don't think they use any more, if they ever did. All I know is that they are big and powerful and rich and they could wipe me out without raising a sweat.'

'And you want me to help you fight them? I think you need more than an English policeman on vacation, Sam.'

'I can't call the cops or the Feds. I can't even tell Collis. If I do they'll send in the choppers.'

'Christ, you make it sound like a war zone.'

'That's what it is,' he said, and he meant it too.

'So how do you think I can help?'

'I'm not sure anyone can but after I've heard their deal, maybe we can talk again.'

'I'll be glad to,' I said, trying to sound convincing.

'Come around tomorrow afternoon.'

'I will.'

'Is there anything you need?'

'If there is, we can talk tomorrow.'

'I'll call the hospital,' he told me. 'Don't worry about the cost.'

I hadn't even thought about it but I suppose the Lewis family soon would; or what was left of them. 'Thanks,' I said.

'You won't talk about this, will you?'

'I'll tell Victoria.'

'Sure, that's okay, but no one else.'

'You've told no one?'

He gestured along the garage towards the men working there. 'Everyone at Laronne knows we're being hit but not the rest of it.'

'Not even your son?'

'Cliff knows some of it, but what can he do? I tell you, Mace, these guys are heavy.'

'Okay,' I said. 'I'll play it all close to my chest.'

He held out a hand and I took it. His

grip was dry and hard. 'Thank you,' he said.

'I haven't done anything yet.'

'It helps to tell someone.'

'That sounds like psychiatrist talk.'

He grinned. 'Maybe Ruth is wearing me down.'

'Does she know any of this?'

'Hell, no. She doesn't even know about the hijacking. This is no business for a woman.'

'Victoria's a woman.'

'She can take care of herself, anyone can see that.'

I hoped he was right. 'I think it's time I went to the hospital.'

'Tell Eddie to give you the Chevy.'

'Thanks.'

Near where we stood was a canvas-sheeted shape. 'What's that?' I asked.

Monahan's face closed up tight. 'Not a damn thing,' he said and turned to walk out of the garage.

I watched him go, then lifted the corner of the canvas. The vehicle beneath the sheet was a sleek and spotless white E-Type Jaguar convertible, maybe a dozen years or more old.

Eddie gave me the keys to a silver Chevrolet. I thought of asking him about the Jaguar but it was no concern of mine and, anyway, Eddie looked as if he would call his boss if I asked him the time.

I did ask if I could borrow a carlift and then spent a while destroying my already half-ruined clothes crawling about under the rental car. I found scraps of wire that told me the explosive charge had been fixed to the wheel strut. It would need a specialist to tell me how it had been detonated and I doubted I would find one this side of the San Francisco police bomb squad.

I scrambled from under the car, dusted off my clothes as best I could and looked up to see Eddie eyeing me curiously. I decided to take a chance that he was loyal to his boss and had no involvement in the attempts on Victoria's life.

'Do you use explosive around here?' I asked.

His expression didn't change while he thought about answering the question. 'Some,' he said eventually, presumably having decided that as I was pally with Sam I could be accommodated just a little.

'What kind?'

'Mostly gelignite.'

'What do you use it for?'

'Re-shaping the land,' he said as if it were a normal everyday event. 'Sometimes we need to alter slopes to improve irrigation, or get the angles right so we pick up more sunlight.'

What Old Ma Nature alone could not do, California's winemakers and some high-explosive would put right. 'Where do you keep it?'

'A cellar beneath the main warehouse.'

'Who has the keys?'

He frowned, looked from me to the damaged car and back again. 'Me and the boss, no one else.'

'Thanks,' I said.

I climbed into the Chevrolet, started the engine and reversed out of the garage. Eddie watched me go, then, while I could still see him, he picked up a wall-mounted telephone and punched three buttons. I guessed he was calling Sam

Monahan to tell him I was interested in explosives. It didn't matter; at least it showed I was right in taking a chance on Eddie's loyalty.

Along the drive I passed a handful of men working on the lawn under floodlights. By dawn, when the red-eyed revellers left the party, there would be no sign left of the crash. I wondered if the memory of what had happened to Linda Lee Lewis would be erased as easily from my mind and was uncomfortably aware that it would not.

8

The hospital was white, the way hospitals are supposed to be. Unlike most others I'd seen this one had Spanish arches, hibiscus and bougainvillaea growing everywhere, and more Rolls Royces in the staff parking lot than seemed decent.

Liverpool has white-painted hospitals, even if the paint peels and discolours somewhat swifter than here, but Spanish architecture and fancy flowers are in short supply. True, there is the occasional Roller to be seen on Merseyside but they tend to keep rolling — just in case.

All the limousines were under flood-lights which gleamed off their immaculate paintwork. Obviously their owners felt neither embarrassment at this display of wealth, nor any danger of retaliation from the not-so-poor and huddled mob whose sickness helped pay their fees.

Victoria and Collis were coming out of the main doors as I arrived. In the bright light bouncing off the walls she looked paler than usual and I hugged her to me for a moment, trying to impart some reassurance. I could tell I wasn't succeeding.

By something approaching a miracle of medicine, the baby's life had been saved although she was hanging on by the barest thread. I felt a momentary pang at being critical of the doctors. Greg Lewis had been knocked out by a combination of chemicals designed to put him on his feet in a few hours.

'I guess someone is turning serious over this,' Collis said.

'It looks that way.'

He frowned, rubbing at his moustache. 'Maybe we should open up the files and see if Peter Raskin has a crazy relative who doesn't like what you did to him.'

Victoria nodded slowly.

'Have you any objections if I ask a few questions around town?' I asked.

Collis thought about that for a while. 'Just so long as you tread softly.'

'I will.'

We left Collis to do whatever the rest of

his night shift entailed and drove to the hotel. The Lewis's camper reminded me of the children and animals. 'What happens to Lewis's kids?' I asked.

'I called Phil Smeeton,' Victoria said. 'He's making sure the minder stays on duty until Greg comes back from the hospital.'

One way and another, all Smeeton's expertise was being tested this week.

We went inside, collected our room key from a bored old man who held down the graveyard shift on the Mount View's desk and went upstairs.

With our damaged and bloodstained clothing piled up ready for disposal and all external signs showered away from our bodies we went to bed. Lovemaking did not seem right, so we just lay there, wrapped together, mostly silent except when I told Victoria of my conversation with Sam Monahan. There were only a few hours left until the sun picked at the window blinds and neither of us slept much.

'Tell me about the killings,' I said, as we dressed. 'You said there were twelve of them, spread over three years.'

'That's right. All were women, mostly aged between twenty and thirty-five. I think there was one who was eighteen and one around forty-five. There was no other connecting factor. Some of them knew one another but that was inevitable in a tight area.'

'How were they killed?'

'No pattern, some were strangled, some beaten to death, one shot, a couple stabbed.'

'What made the local police think it was a serial killer?'

'Desperation, I guess. There didn't seem to be any other explanation.'

'But you found one.'

She nodded her head. 'Most serial killers are also rapists. They rape, sometimes torture, then kill.' Her lips twisted in distaste. 'Sometimes the sequence varies. There are those who kill first, then mutilate and only then commit the sex act.'

'I've read about them. So far we don't seem to have serial killers in Britain.'

'I don't recommend it as an import.

God alone knows how many there are in this country, or how many victims. The estimate is that about five thousand people die each year in this way. Mostly women, but there are those that prey on men.'

'How many are caught?'

'Almost none. The only motive is a desire to rape and kill. They're often drifters, spreading their killings over thousands of miles. Correlating incidents is difficult and, even if it wasn't, there's still nothing to tie them together. Most times, the only way you know if you have a serial killer is if one confesses after he's been picked up on other charges.'

'So what made this case different?'

'For one thing, none of the victims was sexually assaulted.' Victoria was ready to face the world now and her colour had fully returned despite having had so little sleep. She looked even better than usual this morning, standing in the sun-filled room and finishing applying the eye makeup that was about her only concession to artificial aids. She was wearing a slate-grey skirt slim enough to make any movement a provocation to my easily inflamed imagination, and a dusky pink sweater which, while loose, was made of a material that clung to her breasts in a decidedly disconcerting manner. The only thing that was wrong with the scene was the conversation. We should have been talking about our future, not discussing a mass murderer.

'The absence of a sex attack wasn't enough, of course,' she continued. 'More important was a link we found. You see, serial killers rarely know their victims. They pick up hitchhikers, maybe break into a house chosen pretty much at random, meet someone casually in a bar or a supermarket and either make a pick up or trail the woman to her home or to some place where there are no witnesses. So, finding a common factor among the victims means you haven't got a serial killer, but a mass murderer. All but one of the victims had recently lost a close relative, usually their mother, occasionally an aunt or an older sister. That made us think we had a man with local knowledge.'

'How did you tie it all to Raskin?'

'A couple of the victims only moved here after their relative's death so local newspapers wouldn't have carried a report. Death isn't the kind of thing people talk about, but Raskin worked in the Social Security office in St Helena. That's one place where the deaths would be on file. That put him on our list When we cross-checked we found a couple of other things: a partial print at one scene, reported sightings of a car like Raskin's at a couple of locations, one or two other things that wouldn't have been worth a light without the main connecting factor.'

We went down to street level in search of breakfast. I didn't want to say so but it all sounded a shade thin. 'How did Raskin measure up when you interviewed him?'

'He was very nervous, told lies, offered a phoney alibi for the time of some of the killings. Gerry Mandan and I were sure enough to talk to the Sheriff.'

'If Raskin hadn't started shooting would you have nailed him in court?'

'I think he would have cracked under

interrogation or under cross-examination.'

'But if he hadn't?'

We were outside the diner tucked under the hotel and Victoria came to an abrupt halt, glaring at me. 'What are you trying to say? That we didn't have a case?'

'Of course not. I want to learn as much as I can about this. I can't go around town asking questions about what's happening now if I don't know what happened then.'

Victoria calmed down and smiled an apology as we went in to eat.

Over breakfast Victoria filled in a few other odds and ends but nothing appeared especially significant. I came to the conclusion that I would have to knock on doors, ask questions, and wait and see if anything popped. In other words, routine procedure.

Victoria wanted to make the rounds with me but first she decided to drive out to the hospital and see Greg Lewis. I gave her the keys to Sam Monahan's Chevrolet. Calistoga was small enough to get around on foot, at least until I had covered all the offices and stores around Lincoln, its main street.

After she had gone I started my rounds at the newspaper office, then worked my way through the offices of a couple of attorneys, a real estate broker and a cpa. I wasn't expecting miracles. All I wanted was background to what had happened here a decade earlier.

There were no miracles, and neither was there much background. The people I talked to knew very little and certainly didn't want reminding of those days.

I was trying to decide where I should begin some serious questioning when I saw a familiar name on a discreet brass plate beside a door set in between two store fronts. Opening the door I was faced with a flight of stairs and went up them to a large, airy, open-plan office filled with clean-lined blond wood furniture and enough pot plants to generate oxygen for a thousand people.

There were two women in the office. One, the youngest, was sitting facing the head of the stairs and smiled brightly at me. She was unusually thin, with a pointed face and dark hair pulled straight back. She was dressed in a soberly-cut black trouser suit, white shirt and a loosely tied red silk cravat.

'Can I help you?' she asked.

I pointed at her companion who had her back to me and was talking intently on the telephone. The conversation came to an end and as she replaced the phone Ruth Beckerman turned and saw me. She smiled, stood up and came over.

I hadn't looked at her too closely last evening and now I could see that her face was weathered with tiny lines and creases set in by too much outdoor activity. She had a tough and wiry look about her and I guessed that at one time, if not now, she had been something of a sportswoman.

'How are you?' she asked.

'Okay.'

She gestured towards the telephone she had just left. 'That was Sam. He told me what happened. How dreadful. He said something about a baby.'

'Linda Lee was pregnant. The doctors managed to save the baby — a girl. Whether she'll live, I don't know.'

'What a terrible thing. The evening started out as a celebration, yet ended that way.' She shook her head sadly. Glancing at the younger woman, she introduced us.

Jane Cole was a newly-graduated student in her first position. I gained the impression that she thought it pretty special to be employed by Ruth Beckerman, and that the practice was very busy. I have never found anyone who could explain to me the passion so many Americans seem to hold for psychiatry and all its related ologies and isms. I didn't say so, there was nothing to be gained by offending them both.

'There are a couple of things I would like to ask you,' I said. 'Professional advice, you could call it.'

Ruth Beckerman raised an eyebrow sending the network of lines on her forehead into bold relief. 'You surprise me. I would have guessed you were well adjusted.'

I smiled. 'I get by. No, not about me. It's to do with the murders ten years ago.'

'The Raskin murders?'

115

'Yes.'

'Sam told me your friend was on the case.'

'Did you know Raskin?'

'He consulted me,' she said.

All I had hoped for was some general thinking, now it looked as if I'd struck lucky. 'How did he become the way he was?'

'I don't know.'

'Twelve murders need a solid motive, surely?'

'Maybe, maybe not. Once a man begins killing the act itself can become its own motive. He can't stop; he's like an addict or an alcoholic but instead of heroin or booze he's hooked on murder. Killer's wine is how I've heard it described.'

'How about his friends and relatives, how might they think about him now?'

'Now?'

I realised I couldn't play it too close to my chest. 'Would an angry relative take a crack at Victoria while she's here?'

She thought for a moment. 'Several police officers were involved at the end. Most lived around here and some still do.

If someone wanted vengeance there has been ample opportunity in the past nine or ten years.'

But they weren't the ones to fire the shots that killed him, I thought. 'Maybe she was just the last straw, all that was needed to tip the balance of a mind.'

'Who can tell? The longer I live and the more I think I learn about the human mind, the less I understand.' She smiled and rested a hand on the younger woman's shoulder. 'That is not meant to discourage you, my dear, take it merely as a caution.'

Jane Cole smiled up at her boss with an admiring glint in her eye.

'Is whatever made Raskin kill all those women a hereditary condition?' I asked.

'I don't know what made him do it, but while I dislike making generalisations I would think it unlikely. Something in Peter's own past will have provided the spur.'

'So putting that the other way around, there could be a crazy relative trying to kill Victoria, the spur being Raskin's death.'

She pursed her lips. Whatever Ruth Beckerman might be, she wasn't vain. Almost every facial movement she made accentuated her signs of advancing middle-age. 'Possibly,' she said, obviously reluctant to deliver a straight answer. 'But, as I said, the human mind is not easily understood. Peter's death could have provided a spur to someone else's psychosis but I would think it unlikely.'

I was getting nowhere. To be fair, Ruth needed more facts but first I would talk to Victoria. She was the one in the firing line and should have the final say in who was put in the picture.

'Maybe we can talk about this again,' I suggested.

'Of course. Why not call me and you can come over for dinner.' She went to her desk for a business card. 'My home address is on here, too. And do bring Lieutenant Bercovici, won't you.'

I told her I would.

Down on the street I headed for the bookshop and rummaged around until I found their section on psychiatry. It was considerably more extensive than its counterpart would have been in a small-town bookshop in England, but most of the titles meant nothing to me. I glanced through chapter headings, read a few random passages and came to the conclusion that if I read these books I might know all there was to know about myself but I would be no wiser about what turned some men into mass-murderers.

Towards the rear of the store in an area without bookshelves were a couple of small tables, chairs, a coffee machine and a sign which encouraged customers to help themselves. It was eminently civilized and I took up the offer.

A tall blonde lady, young, athletic and very attractive, was stacking books onto shelves not far away. I asked her if she had any suggestions for a book that would give me some insight into the psychology of murderers. She looked at me with considerable curiosity.

'I'm not a freak,' I hastily told her. 'I have a dinner date with an expert and I want to know what she's talking about.

Otherwise conversation will be somewhat stilted.'

She smiled. 'Not exactly what I would choose as a suitable subject over food but . . . ' She dumped an armful of books on the floor and went over to a desk. 'Odd you should ask. This came in today. It's a special order for a customer; sounds exactly what you want. That's why I was curious.'

She showed me the book. She was right, it was precisely the kind of thing I wanted. Written by a professor of criminal psychology at a New York university, it was a plain language guide to a topic where plain language was probably not often used.

Another customer needed assistance and the young woman left me to leaf through the book. I decided to make a note of the title and author and try for a copy at the public library as glancing through it now wouldn't be much use. I had a pen but no paper. There was a pad on the desk and I bent over it to write out the details. As I did so a slip of paper slid from the book. It was a carbon copy of the internal order form giving the name and address of the customer who had ordered the book.

I stood there for a moment, my mind racing while I went through the motions of copying out the title and author of the book on the pad.

For the life of me, I couldn't think of any reason why such a book should not have been ordered by anyone at all. Nevertheless, it was an acute understatement to say that I was curious to know why the psychology of murderers was a subject of interest to old Bill Haigh, the one-armed filling station owner in the derelict township of Vidal.

9

On the way to Vidal Victoria thought of a dozen reasons why Bill Haigh should want to read a book about criminal psychology; all of them entirely plausible and not in any way connected with what was happening to us. But she didn't suggest that we turn back.

Instead of taking the main highway I checked Rand McNally for an alternate route and found one which followed the lake shore, winding among manzanitas and ironwood trees, up and over hills and always within arm's reach of the coming season's crop of grapes.

It was a very pleasant way to spend an afternoon and although neither one of us said so, there was an air of unspoken regret that we couldn't properly enjoy the sights and smells of it all. The real world kept crowding in.

We were almost into Vidal when the road curved suddenly and sharply around a rocky protrusion from the soft soil of the hillside that fell away towards the lake. As we swung around the rock a stationary tanker truck came into view and I braked hard registering several things simultaneously. The tanker, which had the name Laronne painted on it, was slewed half across the narrow road; a man was lying face down in the dirt by the roadside with his hands clasped behind his head; and three other men were clustered around the tail of the truck watching a curving stream of liquid which gushed from it to mingle with the dust before pouring muddily down to the lake.

As we skidded to a standstill the three men turned almost in slow motion. One of them held a gun. While my brain recorded that he had straw-yellow hair I was crashing into reverse, intent on getting out of range. Victoria was too fast for me and flung open her door and went out of the car in a headlong dive towards the protection of the rocky outcrop. I made a despairing grab for her, stalled the motor; and then heard her yelling a warning to the three men. While she was still telling them that she was a police officer and that they should all be good boys and put their hands up, Yellow Hair started shooting while the other two disappeared around the back of the tanker.

A bullet ploughed across the wing of Sam Monahan's Chevrolet but I was more concerned for my own safety than for his property. Restarting the car, I lurched backwards down the road until I was out of the gunman's sight.

I stopped again and left the car to find Victoria. She was wearing green this afternoon and it toned well with the streaks of brown earth that were smeared all over her dress, her arms and legs and her face.

'Did I ever tell you you're beautiful?' I asked as I slid down beside her.

She didn't turn her head. 'Someone is trying to kill us, and you have to make jokes.'

'Who's joking?'

'Dammit, Mace . . . ' Somewhere beyond the tanker an engine roared into life.

Victoria started to scramble to her feet but I pulled her down beside me. 'Leave it, they're not our problem.'

I could tell that she didn't agree but the fading sound of the car engine told her that pursuit was futile.

The man who had been lying on the road was now at the back of the tanker wrestling with a valve and as we came up to him the flow gurgled to a stop. I didn't know what stage of production it came from but there was no doubt that a large quantity of Sam Monahan's wine had been poured away to where it would never again aggravate the livers of imbibers. What it would do to the worms and insects by the lake shore didn't bear thinking about but then, I wasn't too sure if worms even had livers.

'What happened?' Victoria asked him.

The driver was small and dark with a Zapata moustache and a scar across one cheek that would have made him look fierce if he hadn't been frightened out of his wits. 'The bastards stop me on the highway. Make me drive down here and then ... ' He had a strong accent that could have been Mexican.

'What will you do now?'

'This time, most of the load is okay. So, I finish the run.' He glanced up the road in the direction taken by the three men in the car. 'They won't try again.' He didn't sound too sure about that but looked less afraid.

We waited until he had swung the truck around to face back up the road we had come down, then waved him off. 'So, Sam's troubles are real,' I said as the truck disappeared around the rocky outcrop.

I helped Victoria dust off the worst of the dirt before we went back to the car. She ran a finger along the crease made in the Chevrolet's wing by the bullet. 'Was he trying to hit you?' she asked.

I checked the angle. 'Not unless he was the worst shot in the world.'

'I didn't get a good look at any of them, did you?'

The one with the gun and the yellow hair had been tall and well-built with a hard face that had seen surprisingly little sunshine. He was maybe thirty years old.

I would know him again.

It took us another quarter hour to reach Vidal, coming in on a different road to the one I had taken on my first visit.

I drove steadily because there was always the chance the three men would have stopped someplace in order to remonstrate with us for interfering in their little game.

I pulled into the filling station and climbed out as the door opened. Bill Haigh was dressed in the same grease-stiff coverall and wearing the same baseball cap on his bald head.

He grinned as he recognised me, then beamed even more, with open admiration, as Victoria stepped from the car.

He glanced down at the dirty streaks on her clothing, then flicked a sideways look at me that had a decidedly roguish glint to it. 'I hadn't figured you for an open-air man,' he remarked. He held open the door to the diner and Victoria went inside. I followed, debating whether or not to set the record straight. Then I decided against it. Any explanation would open up what had happened along the road and I could see no reason to involve Bill in Sam Monahan's problems. Apart from that, I rather liked the idea of making love to Victoria in the open air with nothing but the heat of the sun on our bodies.

Inside the diner Bill became an attentive and courteous host, insisting on putting on fresh coffee when Victoria told him she didn't want a stronger drink. 'Now it's you who has another fan,' I said.

'Jealous?'

'There's only room for one jealous person in any partnership,' I said.

'Is that what we have? A partnership?'

I could tell that she wasn't making idle conversation.

'You know it's more than that. But, I have to admit, it helps to know that we have so much in common.'

'Like being targets for just about anyone who owns a gun.'

'You know what I mean.'

Bill came back into the room carrying a coffee pot and three extra large mugs wet from what I took to be a hasty wash.

'There you go,' he said, pouring out coffee which smelled good enough to drink. 'Sugar, cream?'

'Sugar, please,' Victoria told him.

The old boy fussed around a little more and I began to think that we had wasted our time coming down here. Any of the possible reasons Victoria had speculated on for him wanting a book on criminal psychology, curious as they might be, had to be better than any involvement in the case we were tentatively reopening.

'Maybe I should fix up the hotel in a hurry,' Bill said.

Victoria looked at me with arched eyebrows but I chose not to enlighten her. 'You may be right,' I said. I hesitated, trying to think of a way to get into the reason for our being here.

'What happened to your clothes?' Bill asked Victoria. He looked a shade embarrassed. 'I shouldn't have made a joke before. How come you're mussed up like that?'

'We had a scrape with another car,' she told him. 'My door wasn't fastened right and I fell out. We were travelling very slowly so I wasn't hurt.'

He weighed up her remark, his eyes on her face all the time. It was obvious that he didn't believe her but he wasn't about to say so. 'Want to clean up?' was all he said.

'Please.'

He pointed. 'Through there, take the first door on the right and excuse the mess. I don't housekeep as often as I should.'

He waited until Victoria had closed the door behind her before turning to me. He didn't speak, just looked enquiringly at me with fierce blue eyes.

'Did a car come through here a few minutes before we arrived?' I asked.

He nodded. 'A grey Buick Regal, moving too fast. Three men inside, one had black hair, one brown, the other yellow.'

I suppose the number of vehicles coming through Vidal are few enough to make every one memorable.

'We had trouble with them.'

'Not just an automobile scrape?'

'No.'

'Mm. But you don't want to talk about it.'

'Best not.'

He thought about that for a moment. 'It's your business.'

We sat in silence for a moment. I looked at his grandfather's apprenticeship certificate on the wall and tried to think of a way to introduce the book he had ordered from Calistoga. Then he made it easy for me.

'You haven't come back here to admire the view,' he said.

I shook my head. 'Next time, maybe.'

'And this time?'

There was no point in nibbling around the edges. 'You ordered a book from a store in Calistoga.'

He studied me for a long, silent age, then slowly nodded his head. 'It's not against the law.'

'It's an unusual book.'

'Maybe.'

'Any particular reason?'

'Any particular reason for asking?'

I hesitated, then Victoria came back into the room.

The afternoon sun struck in low through the window catching her slightly from behind so that it glowed around her. She was breathtaking; I couldn't let anything happen to her. If I hurt Bill Haigh's feelings it was just too bad. 'Someone is trying to kill Victoria. We don't know who and we're checking everyone.'

He frowned, looked from me to her and back again. 'Sounds a thin lead,' he said.

'It is,' I agreed. 'The trouble is, we haven't much to go on so everything counts.'

'I don't want to cause trouble for anyone,' he said. He looked at Victoria again. 'But I don't want to bring any hurt to you either. The book isn't for me. Someone asked me to place the order. He didn't want anyone in Calistoga to know it was for him.'

'Why not order it in another town?' Victoria asked.

Bill shrugged, the movement awkward with his powerful but lop-sided shoulders. 'I guess we didn't think of that.'

'Who is he?'

He hesitated a moment, then reached a decision. 'You people are cops, aren't you?'

'Yes, we are, but right now this is personal.'

'Okay, I'm a pretty good judge of people and I reckon you'll give Gil a fair shake.'

'Gil?'

'Gil Raskin, he's the guy who ordered the book.'

I looked at Victoria who was frowning at the old man. She caught my look. 'Peter Raskin's brother,' she said.

'Hey, now, are you saying this is connected with that old business?' Bill cut in.

I let Victoria answer him. 'Maybe,' she said.

'No, you have to be wrong. Gil's a harmless guy; he'd never hurt anyone.'

'That's what people said about his brother.'

'I never knew him, but I know Gil.'

'How do you know him?' I asked.

The old man removed his cap and

rubbed at his bald head. He was wrestling with a decision. 'Gil rents a cabin down by the lake. Sometimes he comes alone and fishes, other times he ... ' He paused, then continued. 'Other times he brings a lady friend with him.'

'Who?'

'I've never met her.'

'When was he here last?'

The old man looked uncomfortable. 'He's here now,' he said eventually.

10

The cabin Gil Raskin was using was one of maybe a dozen spread over about a mile and a half of lakeside. Like all the structures around Vidal, they were delapidated affairs made from once-sturdy logs that had split and warped over the years. Tar-paper and plywood covered the worst gaps and discoloured plastic sheet hung over the windows, most of which were broken.

A barely visible track led through the woods behind the cabins and a gold-coloured Charger was parked at the back of the cabin Bill had reluctantly identified. The car was twin to that parked outside the Mount View Hotel the previous morning; given the circumstances I wouldn't have fallen over with shock if it turned out to be the same one. Certainly it was enough to make me question Bill's claim that Gil wouldn't harm anyone.

We split up, Victoria checking the car before covering the back of the cabin. I went down to the lakeside, then worked my way up towards the cabin's front door. There wasn't much cover and I had to crouch low among some spindly shrubs, eventually crawling the last few yards. Iron Eyes Cody would've hired me on the spot.

It was a wasted effort because the cabin was empty. There were just two rooms; one, large, served as a living and sleeping area with a curtained-off alcove housing a tiny kitchen, the other was a small bathroom. The furniture was basic and not very clean although a couple of touches showed that someone used the place regularly. Flowers in a jug drooped but had yet to spill their petals onto the table top. Some brightly coloured lounging pillows looked sufficiently out of place to suggest they hadn't come with the rest of the pioneer-grade decor.

The door leading out to the back was well bolted and looked as though it hadn't been opened since Davy Crockett killed his first hat so I turned to go out the way I'd come in.

I completed the turn but I didn't go outside. Both barrels of a shotgun, held at eye-level and no more than six inches from the bridge of my nose made it clear that movement was something to be avoided at all costs.

I did what the manual tells you to do in such circumstances. I froze. The manual doesn't tell you whether or not to close your eyes but I reached that decision on my own.

'Who in hell are you, mister?' a thin, youngish, but shaky voice demanded.

I risked opening one eye, hoping he wouldn't take it as a sign of aggression. He was tall but not as tall as me; heavy-set but not as much as me; he was pushing forty, the same as me. In normal circumstances I could have taken him without raising a sweat. The circumstances were not normal and I was sweating. His hair was sandy and a cluster of freckles marked the bridge of his nose.

'Gil Raskin?' I enquired, keeping my voice politely low. That's in the manual too.

'Who're you?'

'My name's Mace,' I told him.

That seemed to ring a far-off bell. 'What're you doing here?'

'Just passing through so I thought I'd drop in and talk to you about . . . your boy.' At least my brain was working.

'My boy?'

'You know about the pot-shot he took through my hotel window, don't you?'

'You're the guy?'

At the doorway behind Raskin a shadow flickered by.

'I'm the guy,' I agreed.

He frowned, thinking hard. I had an impression that normal thought processes didn't come easily to him. The shadow at the door hardened. Victoria was a half-pace inside the cabin. I tried not to look at her, a task made easy by my difficulty in seeing past the end of the shotgun. Then Victoria made a sudden, silent movement and a split-second later something clattered against the side wall of the cabin. Whatever it was she had thrown, a stone maybe, didn't make much noise but Raskin was so tense he

138

would have popped if a cricket had chosen that moment to rub its legs together.

He jerked the gun sideways and I let go with a straight left that would have taken his head off his shoulders if it had made the right contact. It didn't because the shotgun roared, jerking him backwards and my punch scraped where it should have broken bones. I took a hopeful grab at the weapon and was taken by surprise when it came my way without resistance. It was almost enough to get me killed. Raskin still had a finger on the second trigger and the barrel was swinging towards my head.

Then Victoria stepped forward and hit him once, hard, on the side of the neck with the barrel of her Smith & Wesson. He went down like the ape in those Clint Eastwood movies, fast and hard.

'Thanks,' I said.

She was looking down at Raskin. 'Any time,' she said, but her voice wasn't making light of it.

I reached out and held her to me. 'I think I love you,' I told her.

Her voice was muffled against my chest. 'I bet you say that to all the girls who save your life,' she said.

'At moments like this, I think I'd say it even if you were a feller.'

She lifted her face and let me kiss her. 'Aren't you glad I'm not,' she said when I let her breathe again.

There were several ways to answer that but then Gil Raskin groaned and the real world elbowed in on us.

The scatter from the shotgun had not improved the decor inside the cabin. Among the casualties was the flower jug which was now in countless pieces. The flowers had vanished.

I helped Gil Raskin to the bed and he sat on the edge, head hanging forward, his shoulders slumped. The mark where Victoria had hit him was red and already showing signs of bruising. By morning he would feel as if he'd gone ten rounds with Marvin Hagler.

'What do you want?' he asked, his voice dull, his head still hanging.

'To talk,' I told him. 'There was no need for the shotgun.'

'Talk? What about?'

'You, your brother.'

His head came up with a jerk and he clutched at his neck. 'My brother?'

'Peter.'

He looked from me to Victoria, his hand still clasped to his neck. 'He's dead.'

'We know that.'

'So why do you want to talk about him?'

'Just to clear up a few things,' I said.

'Denny, my kid, he didn't shoot at you, mister. He told me and Denny doesn't lie.'

'Okay,' I said agreeably.

'About Peter,' Victoria said. 'Were you close to him?'

Raskin's face darkened and after a moment I realised he was blushing. It seemed an odd reaction. 'Pretty close,' he said.

'I don't recall seeing you at the time.'

Raskin looked at her in surprise. 'You were here?'

She ignored the question. 'Where were you?'

'I was working up in Oregon. I came

141

down for the funeral, liked it here and stayed.' He paused but seemed to want to say more. 'My wife wouldn't move down. We split up about a year later. That's why Denny and Sharon are wild. I can't do all I maybe should.' He hesitated again. 'My wife wouldn't take them. They would be in the way. She likes a good time.'

'How often did you visit your brother?' Victoria asked.

'I didn't. The funeral was the first time I came down.'

'You said you were close.'

'They came to visit us.'

'They?'

'Peter and . . . Karen.'

He seemed to have difficulty in speaking his sister-in-law's name. A flicker of light emerged at the edge of my brain. 'Who comes here with you?' I asked.

He looked down at the ground again, the flush spreading along his neck.

'You and Karen?'

He nodded.

'Why the secrecy? She's a widow, you're separated.'

'It's the way Karen wants it.' He didn't sound happy about the way he had to lead his life.

'Tell me about the books you read.' I said.

He looked up again, surprise evident on his face. 'Books?'

I nodded, waiting.

'I don't have much time for reading. I read a Breaker magazine every month. Sometimes I look at *Reader's Digest*, that's about all.'

I took out the paper I'd written on in the Calistoga bookshop and read aloud the title of the book Bill Haigh had ordered.

'How do you know about that?' he asked.

'Just tell me why you ordered the book.'

'Karen still talks about Peter. She doesn't think he killed all those women. She thinks the police made a mistake.' I didn't look at Victoria. 'A few weeks ago, it would have been their twentieth wedding anniversary. She was very down. I tried talking about him but it

143

made things worse. That was when I thought, if I could learn something about how . . . well, how Peter's mind worked, I could maybe help her more than I do.'

'You think he did it, then,' I said.

'I don't know.' He looked up at me, his face working with his thoughts. Obviously Gil Raskin was not the brightest man in the world. It also seemed probable that the book, which had been our only lead, was a waste of time.

'Did Karen ever talk to Peter's doctor and psychiatrist?' I asked.

Raskin looked up at me questioningly. 'There was nothing to learn. Peter was a pretty tough guy and kept in shape especially after he quit his music job in 'Frisco.'

'So he never saw a doctor?'

'Maybe once or twice, but nothing serious and I never heard about any psychiatrist.'

We left Gil Raskin in his cabin, taking care to carry his spare shotgun shells with us. Outside, Bill Haigh was propping up a tree a short distance away.

He also had a shotgun, single barrel, resting in the crook of his arm.

'I heard a shot,' he remarked as we joined him. 'But when I looked in you were all talking kind of friendly so I didn't butt in.'

'That's right,' I said. 'We couldn't be friendlier.'

'I told you he was harmless.'

'So you did.'

'Much damage done in there?'

'Nothing that can't be put right with a few dollars.' I started to reach for my wallet but Bill shook his head.

'No need for that. Places aren't worth a damn anyway.'

We walked slowly back towards the filling station and diner. Victoria hadn't said a word since we came out of the cabin and it wasn't one of those comfortable silences we had discovered we could share. Something was troubling her.

She didn't come out with it until we were in the car and heading back along the lakeshore road. 'I think I should make this enquiry official,' she said.

'This is a holiday,' I said. 'And it's one with a purpose.'

She rested a hand on my leg, too high for my peace of mind. 'I know, but we can't ignore any of this and there's a limit to what I can do unofficially.'

I lifted her hand and kissed it. 'Okay,' I said, smiling at her. 'Ruth Beckerman invited us to dinner at her place some time. I think we should take her up on it. There are a few things we need to know, among them why Peter Raskin was a patient of hers.'

We had reached the rock where the Laronne tanker had been ambushed and the sun which was now low in the west was already drying up the earth. Beyond the rock we had a superb view across the lake.

'Pull over,' Victoria said.

I did as she asked and shut off the motor.

'I want you to make love to me,' she said.

'Here? Now?'

'For God's sake, Mace, don't sound so surprised about it. What's wrong with here and now?' Without giving me a chance to argue one way or the other, she opened the car door and by the time I was outside she was walking down to the water's edge.

She had disappeared from my sight before I was more than halfway down the slope.

'Over here.' Her voice was low and husky.

She had found a small, flat area covered with soft, springy grass and completely sheltered from the view of anyone other than a passing boatman. There were no boats on the lake so we were unobserved. Victoria was already taking off her clothes.

'What was all that about giving up sex in the open air?' I asked.

'There's a time and place, and this is both,' she said.

I decided against arguing; not that I could have thought up any reason for not going along with her mood. The sun, although low, was still hot; we were out of sight; the ground looked comfortable; and, by any standards, I was ready.

When we sank to the wild grass I was having difficulty holding myself in check but this time I had to. So far there had been too much haste in what little lovemaking we'd been allowed.

So we didn't make haste; and we certainly did not simply screw. It really was making love. Slow and languorous and totally satisfying. There was no part of our bodies that was too remote or too secret for fingers and tongues and lips to explore and open up to the soft light of day.

I don't know how long we were there, on that tiny patch of ground by the lake. It couldn't have been anything less than an hour, it might even have been two. There had never been any doubt in my mind that we had no problems in being suited this way; that much had been evident last year. Nor was I naïve enough to think this was all that counted. But the way it was on this particular afternoon and on this special patch of Californian soil made it clear that any number of incompatabilities in other things would be easily overcome.

'I don't think I can stand much more of that,' I said eventually.

Victoria rolled over onto her stomach and looked at me out of the corner of her eye. 'If you mean that then I'm calling it off right now. I don't want you under false pretences. Everything we do now we'll do after we're married and as often as I want it.'

'Did I ever tell you I hate domineering women?'

'I'm sorry.' she said with a not very good attempt at sounding meek.

'Anyway, what was all that about after we're married? I haven't asked you yet.'

She grinned at me. 'Ever hear of equal opportunities in your country? I just gave you a sample.'

'So, we're going to do it?'

She nodded, her face abruptly solemn. 'I think we are.'

'In that case, all we have to decide is whether we choose California or England.'

'I've never been to England so it's an unequal choice for me.'

'Whichever we decide one of us will

have a hard time getting work. I don't expect the LAPD to be too eager to hire an Englishman and my Chief Constable isn't wild about women in the first place, let alone an American.'

'We could both quit our jobs and make love all day.'

I kissed her. 'Great idea and if I was nineteen I would probably agree with you.'

'And how do you see it from the standpoint of your advanced years?'

'I'd be dead in a month.'

Victoria was thinking. 'We could set up a private agency. We're both good at our work and there's no shortage of people needing a private detective.'

It had a nice sound to it; being a private eye in California would be a way of living out a few of my childhood fantasies. Philip Marlowe was alive and well and living deep in my heart. 'Could I get a licence?' I asked.

'I could, right away. You might have problems. I'm not sure, I'll have to look up the statute.'

I didn't answer, I was too busy thinking

about my career in Liverpool. There, I was successful; here, I would be starting over again. There, my life was empty; here, I would have Victoria.

'You're not arguing,' she said quietly. 'Is that because I'm rushing you?'

I put my arms around her and pulled her over on top of me. The afternoon was turning chill and I could feel her skin's response to the fall in temperature. 'Yes, you are and I don't mind one little bit. I think you're right. We get married and we live in California. I'll have to go home, resign, go through all the moves, then come back. I could make it before the end of the summer.'

She buried her face against my chest and something like a shiver ran through her body. As she pressed down on me I began to respond.

Raising her head she looked into my eyes. 'Really?'

'Really.'

She eased away from me and turned to run her mouth down my chest and stomach until she was able to prove for herself that I really was ready again. After what we had done since coming down from the car this was something for the record books. This time we had to be silent as our mouths were in use but a pair of blue jays shrieked with outrage and several fish plopped out of the lake to take lessons.

It was more than another half hour before finally, reluctantly, we dressed and walked hand in hand back up to the car.

'If only to preserve what's left of my masculine pride I think I should tell you that I love you and want to marry you and even if you are turning out to have an unsuspected macho streak in you, I reckon we could make it. At least for long enough until we're both too old to be any use to anyone else.'

'My God, Mace, for a minute there I thought you were about to be genuinely romantic but you had to spoil it.'

'Like I said, I have to protect my pride.'

'Men,' she said, but she sounded happy and so was I.

11

We headed for Laronne, having decided it was late enough in the day to maintain my promise to call on Sam Monahan and hear the outcome of his meeting with the heavy mob.

In the fading light the big house looked no more real than it had with all its party trimmings. It was the kind of house in which Mrs Danvers would have had a whale of a time.

Sam was in his gun-room and he had already learned about our intervention in the hijack attempt. He spent some time thanking us but his mind was on other things.

'Did they come?' I asked.

'They came.' He poured sizable measures of Wild Turkey for us all but his was clearly more medicinal than social.

'What do they want?'

'A share in my business, one drawn up by lawyers, all official, giving them the right to cream off half of everything we make before taxes. If I agree, I'll be working for the bastards for what's left of my life and by the time I'm dead there'll be nothing left to hand on. Not from my share, anyway. They'll own it all.' He picked up the bourbon bottle again, then changed his mind and set it down with a decisive crack. 'I'm not taking this lying down. I mean to fight these bastards.' He hesitated, looking at each of us in turn. 'But I know I need all the help I can get.'

The telephone rang and he glared at it, irritated by the interruption. 'I really could do with some help,' he continued quietly.

Picking up the phone he listened for a moment, then said, 'Yes', replaced the instrument and walked heavily across the room to the door. 'I'll be back in a couple of minutes,' he said. 'Help yourself to the booze.'

'What do you think?' Victoria asked as the door closed behind the stocky little man.

'What can we do? And, anyway, we have enough to handle.'

'Yes, but, like you said, Monahan has pull around here. That could help us.'

'Not so much pull that he can't be put in a sweat-box by a handful of thugs.'

'These people don't sound to me like ordinary thugs. If it is the Organisation they can do all he says and more. Maybe that's what they plan on doing, anyway.'

'Why?'

'Maybe they picked him because he's a feisty little bastard who'll fight and lose. That way they can show the rest of the valley they mean business. We're talking billions of dollars in land values, capital assets, trading. The kind of money that attracts the Mob. It could be that Monahan is just a means to bigger ends.'

If she was right it sounded like a good reason to keep our distance. Tangling with an outfit capable of laying waste to the Napa Valley when we were hunting for a man out to kill Victoria would put us between the rock and the hard place.

Monahan came back, looking questioningly at us. 'The Chevy took a bullet,' he said.

I nodded.

'I guess I really do owe you. Maybe I shouldn't ask you to get involved.'

'We'll do what we can,' Victoria said firmly.

I sighed. 'Okay, I give in. But there are conditions. If there is any conflict of interest, we drop you fast even if it hurts you more than these people can hurt you.'

Monahan gave a decisive nod of his head. 'I would expect that.' He glanced at Victoria. 'And I can't say I blame you, if I'd met a woman like . . . ' He broke off abruptly and turned back to me. 'You said conditions, what are the others?'

I gestured towards the display of handguns. 'Just one. I want one of these.' I glanced at Victoria. 'I take it you won't split on me for carrying a weapon without a permit?'

'I'll do more than that, I'll talk to my chief and have him pull strings.'

'You'll tell him about this?' Monahan asked, suddenly wary.

'I don't have to tell him anything. We have cause enough as it is,' she said.

'Thanks,' Monahan said. He turned to

me. 'Take whatever you want.'

I picked up a Smith & Wesson .32, similar to the one Victoria carried but a six-shot. 'This will be okay, we can share ammunition.'

'It's yours,' Monahan said. He rummaged in a cupboard and came up with a snap-in holster which I clipped to my belt. Monahan handed over a couple of boxes of ammunition and would have provided more but I stopped him. If I used up two boxes of shells we would be in so much trouble that all the firepower in the world wouldn't help us.

'How many men came to see you today?' I asked.

'Three.'

'Can you describe them?'

He grinned. 'I'll do better than that. Eddie put a tail on them. By tonight I'll have names and addresses. You'l have them in the morning.'

'Unless Eddie's man comes back with his ears in his mouth.'

'It's only a tail job,' he said, but his confidence had faded along with his smile.

We drove away from Monahan's house in silence. I took the long driveway down past the trees and the place where Linda Lee had been bloodily speared.

'Don't think about it,' Victoria said, instinctively reading my mind once more.

'If you keep getting into my thoughts this way I'll have to think seriously about separate rooms.'

'Just try it,' she said and we dropped unpleasant subjects.

We covered a few miles of the highway before Victoria spoke again. When she did it was decidedly prosaic but I agreed with her. I too was hungry. Sally Morgan's restaurant seemed like a good idea but it required some map-reading first. I pulled over to check the Rand McNally and wound down the window to let the breeze take over from the air-conditioning. As I did so the sound of gunfire echoed in the distance.

I twisted in my seat. A spread of bright light coloured the sky to the west. It hadn't been there before I stopped the car, I was sure.

I started the motor and was pulling

away before I had thought much about what I was doing. The chances were this had nothing to do with us; every gunshot in California didn't automatically involve what we were mixed up in. On the other hand, years of training made certain reactions instinctive.

The lights were over behind a rise in the ground and as the Chevrolet topped the brow of the hill everything was laid out before us in sharp detail. Three men were clustered around a four-wheel drive truck, one held a rifle and was aiming across the wing towards a broken-down hut inside which I could just make out the shape of another man.

I had hit the brakes and was already reaching for the door handle when other details registered in my mind and I began to laugh.

As the car slid to a standstill in a cloud of dust the men around the jeep stood up, turning towards us with mildly curious expressions on their faces. As they did so the lights dimmed and others came on. These were much less bright and were aimed differently. In their beams the cameras and the film crew were clearly visible.

Far from arriving in the nick of time to rescue someone from being shot to pieces by superior forces, we had butted into a film unit on night-time location.

12

The crew was shooting an episode of *Harper's Valley* and, fortunately, the director had called 'cut' just as we came over the rise and as the rifle shots were to be re-dubbed anyway we hadn't caused a problem.

As technicians started dismantling lamps and camera rails and all the other odds and ends required by film-makers, I began to slide back into the car from which I had all but emerged in true TV cop style. Then I caught a glimpse of a face I recognised. Holly Monahan wasn't looking quite as spectacular as she had at her father-in-law's house. The red dress which had fitted her like a second skin had been replaced by tailored denims and a soft suede–leather sleeveless jacket worn over a check shirt. On her feet she wore hand-tooled cowboy boots that would have had Dale Evans green with envy. Holly recognised me too and walked over with a welcoming smile coming onto her face.

Tonight, it seemed, was her first appearance on the set and although she didn't say so I could tell that she was nervously anxious to impress. The fact that we had turned up when we did gave her a chance to talk to someone outside the company, all of whom were total strangers. We were not much better than that, but it didn't stop her from talking excitedly until, abruptly, she ran out of adrenalin and decided that she needed a drink.

'Join me?' she asked.

'Thanks,' I said and looked at Victoria in time to meet a withering glare. I grinned at her, made a big show of taking Holly's arm, and we all headed for a trailer which appeared to serve as dressing-room, bar and, judging from the size of a couch which spread across the rear end, several other things besides, none of which I risked thinking about.

We had barely put our noses into the glasses of Jim Beam which Holly poured out, without asking our preferences in the matter, when we were joined by the director, a bearded thirty-year-old with the rounded shoulders and worry lines of a man accustomed to living on the edge of panic.

He congratulated Holly on her first day's work, accepted a glass of bourbon with a distracted smile, then finally focussed on Victoria and me. I don't know what I did for him but Victoria certainly lightened his burden. He took some convincing that she wasn't in the same business as he was, or a model, or anything glamorous. By this time, there seemed little point in keeping secret who we were. Too many people already knew and, anyway, Holly would either know or soon find out through her family connections.

'A cop?' the director said, staring at Victoria's face. Then he managed to unhook his eyes and took in the fact that she wasn't especially immaculate today. 'Jesus, maybe you are.' He shook his head and sipped heavily at his drink. 'With cops like you, who needs actors?' He flicked a quick glance at Holly and added a lifesaver. 'Present company excepted, of course.'

'Of course,' Holly said. Her smile suggested she wasn't taking him too seriously. She had no worries anyway and she must have known it. Although still only in her early twenties, she was smart enough to have learned the effect her appearance would have on her life.

The director finished his bourbon, handed the empty glass to Holly and turned to the door. Glancing back, he smiled uncertainly at her. 'How're you getting on with Chuck?'

'No problems,' Holly said.

He nodded. 'Glad to hear it.' He opened the door. 'Speak of the devil,' he added, stepping to one side to admit another man.

The newcomer was medium height with wide shoulders and a deep chest that made his legs look inadequate to take his bulk. He had tightly curled grey hair above a heavy face whose thickish lips and cheeks had a purple glow suggesting an overfondness for Old John B. Once upon a time he had been very good-looking. I knew that because I recognised him; he was Charles Gatliff, a movie actor who had once guaranteed a queue at my local fleapit but who had all but disappeared from sight until he turned up as the star of *Harper's Valley*. On the small screen, made up for his role as the patriarch of a rich family with more money than a couple of hundred Sam Monahans added together, he still looked good. In real life, however, he looked like an ageing, overweight drunk.

'Ah, there you are, Barry,' he said to the director in a near-English accent. Obviously he wasn't doing it for my benefit, maybe he thought he was Cary Grant. 'My first scene tomorrow is causing me a little trouble.'

The director looked at him blankly.

'When I arrive at the house,' Gatliff added helpfully.

'For Christ's sake, Chuck, all you do is drive up, get out of the car, and walk into the house. Where's the difficulty?'

'My motivation,' Gatliff explained. 'What's my motivation?'

The director stared at him in amazed

silence for a moment. 'Chuck,' he said, carefully suppressing the mounting hysteria that showed in his eyes, 'as you drive up in the car you are thinking 'Where the fuck am I going in this car?' When you get out of the car and walk into the house you are thinking 'How the fuck did I get here?' Okay?'

Gatliff frowned in concentration, apparently hearing nothing exceptional in the director's words or tone of voice. 'Thank you, Barry,' he said. 'It really is a pleasure to work with you.'

'It's Gary,' the director said. 'Not Barry.' He went out, slamming the trailer door with unnecessary violence.

Holly announced that she intended taking a shower and disappeared through a door down towards the far end of the trailer. Gatliff helped himself to a drink, looking quite at home. He didn't look at us, so we left. I think Cary Grant would at least have said 'Goodbye'.

We had covered only a few paces across the dusty ground outside the trailer when I saw someone else I recognised. It was starting to feel like old home week. I slipped an arm around Victoria's waist and slowed her down. 'See the guy over there, near the jeep?'

It was the young motor cycle cop I had seen as I drove through the fog. The same one who hadn't told me about Bill Haigh's filling station. I told Victoria who he was.

'What about him?'

'I'd like to know why he lied about Bill Haigh.'

'Haven't we enough to worry about?'

'I'm a compulsive question asker.'

'Now you tell me.'

'Anyway, there's a chance he knows about Gil Raskin using the cabin at the lake.'

'I thought we had ruled him out.'

'We have, but until we have a limitless list of suspects we'll have to keep raking over those we think didn't do it.'

'Is that how you investigate crime in Liverpool?'

'Not usually,' I acknowledged.

The young cop was talking with a group of technicians and was now heading towards a row of trucks.

A thick-necked man in the denims and check shirt that appeared to be the standard form of dress around here came towards me looking grim in the remaining lights. 'Is that your car?' he asked.

He meant the Chevrolet so I admitted ownership. 'Move it, will you? We have to roll these trucks out of here tonight.' He wandered off, muttering to himself about overtime rates.

'I'll move the car over to Holly's trailer,' I told Victoria. 'You keep an eye on the cop.'

'Not too close to the trailer,' she warned.

By the time I had moved the car Victoria was out of sight and so too was the young cop and the men he had been with. Most of the lights were being disconnected now and the site was growing darker by the moment. I was standing by the door of the car, fumbling a key into the lock when I heard Holly's voice. The words were indistinguishable but there was no mistaking their mood. She was very angry.

It wasn't any business of mine, but I

went back to the trailer all the same. At the door I could hear her words now. 'You're drunk, Chuck,' she was saying. 'So why not go back to the hotel, sleep it off like a good boy, and tomorrow we can talk about it all over lunch.'

The man spoke but his words were a meaningless rumble. Then something shattered and Holly screamed, a small, tight sound maybe, but a scream for all that. I opened the door and went inside.

Holly was standing in the middle of the trailer. Her short blonde hair was wet and so too were her arms and shoulders. From there on down she was largely covered by a huge towel which was a similar red to the dress she had worn at Laronne. Her feet were wet too and marking the carpeted floor.

Gatliff was crouching, trying clumsily to gather up pieces of broken glass. He had dropped a tumbler and from the state of the carpet it had been full; I guessed it wasn't the one he'd poured earlier.

He twisted his head around, looking up at me. 'What the hell do you want?' he demanded, the words blurring at the edges.

'Hello, Holly,' I said, ignoring him.

There was relief on her face. 'Hi,' she said brightly, as if men were always walking in on her when she was wearing nothing but a bath towel. 'I'll be ready in a moment. Chuck's just leaving. You didn't really meet, did you?'

Chuck and I looked at one another; I had the impression I was about to make another enemy but from somewhere he pulled a smile in which I could see vestiges of the one I had seen grinning down from posters. 'Delighted to meet you, old boy. Any friend of Holly's is a friend of mine, eh.' The English accent was better this time.

He found a bin and managed to put most of the glass into it before heading for the door. 'See you around, old chum,' he said and went out into the night.

'Was I pleased to see you come through that door,' Holly said. I smiled at her. 'I could do with a drink,' she added and moved towards the bar. Then she squealed, almost fell, and let the towel slip to the floor. She didn't seem to notice she was now completely naked. Instead, she was busily inspecting her right foot. A tiny drop of blood gleamed on the heel where I guessed she had stepped on a sliver of glass.

'Let me look,' I said.

Obligingly, she flopped onto the bed, holding her foot up for inspection still seemingly unmindful that the action showed me everything that her mother should have warned her to keep covered. I couldn't find any glass in the cut but I have to admit I wasn't giving it the attention I was supposed to. Reaching for the towel I handed it to her.

'Really?' she asked.

I nodded slowly. 'Really.'

'She is beautiful,' she said, taking the towel and wrapping it across her breasts but still leaving herself dangerously vulnerable from the waist down. Her pubic hair was surprisingly dark because her blonde hair looked real.

'Yes, she is,' I agreed. 'Also, she's likely to walk in through that door any minute now.'

She grinned cheekily. 'We could lock it.'

'Don't tempt me,' I said, then pulled the towel across to shut out the delights that would have to remain hidden if my blood pressure was to stay on the scale.

Standing up she kissed me, reaching up to do it and letting the towel slip again. She let it lay where it fell and walked across to the shower room, well aware that from behind she was just as tempting as from the front. 'Wait until I dress, will you. Please. Chuck's notorious. He's probably hiding outside, waiting to see if you leave without me.'

'Okay,' I agreed, listening to the blood in my ears.

She took longer than she had any right to, and somehow managed to find the need to walk backwards and forwards across the trailer looking for garments and only very gradually putting them on.

I listened to the sounds of vehicles starting up and driving around the site, the occasional yells of men as they loaded trucks, and tried not to think too much about Holly Monahan. In fact, it wasn't as hard as I would once have thought.

Victoria was turning me into a one-woman man. And I was also aware that I needed to get out of there and find out how she was getting on with the motor cycle cop.

When Holly was finally ready she wore a light-green woollen dress pulled in at the waist with a gold chain. With matching gold-coloured very high-heeled sandals, she contrived to look sexily demure.

'Cliff's coming over to collect me,' she announced. 'He should be here soon.'

Lucky Cliff, I thought. 'How long have you been married?'

'A year and a half.' She smiled at me with frank open-ness. 'Don't get any wrong thoughts. Cliff and I are happy but I have a career that takes me away a lot of the time and when I'm down in LA, or maybe in New York, or sometimes Hawaii you can't expect me to act like a nun, can you?'

I didn't answer. It wasn't my problem. If it had been, I would have had an answer for her but she wouldn't have liked it.

'I have to leave,' was what I did say. 'Will you be okay if Gatliff comes back?'

She nodded, clearly sorry to see me go.

I opened the door, glanced outside, then felt a sudden snatch of concern. Sam Monahan's Chevrolet had gone. It surely hadn't been stolen. Victoria must have taken it, but why? Had she come back and seen me in the trailer with the naked Holly? Or had the young cop done something that needed prompt action. Maybe, unable to find me, Victoria had taken off on her own. Whichever way it was, there was nothing for me to feel happy about.

There could have been other reasons for Victoria and the car not being here, of course, but I had even less desire to think about them.

13

I was still spinning on the spot, trying not to panic, when Cliff Monahan arrived to take his wife home. Begging a ride from a man whose wife had been showing me her all a few minutes earlier was not something I would normally have done but I couldn't afford to be choosy.

'Where do you want to be?' he asked.

I didn't know but Calistoga seemed like a good place to start. The young cop might not have any direct connection with the town but Deputy Collis would either know him or be able to identify and, hopefully, locate him for me.

Cliff drove too fast but he seemed to know the roads and his slate-grey Cadillac Seville whisked along without incident. That he could drive at all was mildly miraculous because Holly, sitting in the front passenger seat, did everything but crawl onto his lap. Whether it was to cover up a feeling of guilt, or to impress me, or that she was simply randy, I don't know. I do know that at another time and in another place, I would have arrested the pair of them.

'The old man tells me you're on the payroll,' Cliff remarked as he slid the big car between one of the TV company's vehicles and a panel-truck coming the other way without actually scraping paint.

I decided that travelling with my eyes closed might be the answer. 'Not exactly,' I said. 'I'll ask a few questions, look around, that's all. And there's no money in it.'

That surprised him. 'I didn't think anyone did anything for free any more.'

'I'm one of nature's gentlemen.' I risked opening my eyes and intercepted a glance from Holly. Her grin told me that she really believed I was. 'How much do you know?' I asked him.

'Most of it, I guess. Old Sam doesn't keep secrets from his son and heir.' He smiled over his shoulder at me. 'If those guys make trouble and ruin the business then I'm the one who loses most. I could end up inheriting nothing more valuable than Sam's gun collection.'

'Have you met them?'

'I saw them arrive and leave but they wanted their negotiations in private.' His voice was flat, not giving me any clue how he thought about it.

'What do you think Sam should do?' I asked.

'Fight, what else?'

His voice was not as strong as the words he was using. I studied the back of his head from my seat at the rear of the Cadillac. He seemed an amiable character, not wholly caught up in the race for money which appeared to motivate the guests at Laronne the night Linda Lee Lewis died. But amiability and lack of lust for loot, while more acceptable traits of character than many I could think of, were not the weapons needed to fight Sam Monahan's enemies.

I didn't say so; maybe Cliff was trying to impress Holly, maybe he thought it was the right thing to say, maybe he really meant it.

'The name Laronne,' I said. 'You mentioned someone called Laraine, is

177

that where it comes from?'

He didn't answer right away. 'Yes,' he said eventually. 'My mother was called Laraine, so was my step-mother. I think that was why Sam married her, because of her name.' There was a new note in his voice.

'What happened to her?'

'My mother died when I was born.' Cliff's tone was bleak and I could tell I was at the edges of a very private part of his life even if that had not been my intention.

'I meant the second Laraine,' I said.

'She died too.'

The big car surged forward as he pressed down on the accelerator. There was no need for more speed. We were already travelling faster than was safe. My questions were the cause. Then, abruptly, he slowed to a pace more likely to let us live a while longer.

'She drove pretty fast,' Cliff said. 'And she flew the executive jet, went surfing, even tried free-fall parachuting. Christ, she certainly knew how to pack everything in. Sometimes . . . ' His voice trailed away, then picked up again and I knew that he was no longer talking for my benefit. 'Sometimes I think she knew she wouldn't be around for ever and wanted to cram in everything she could before the end.'

'How did she die?' I asked quietly.

'She put the jet into a fast turn, stalled it and went into the side of a mountain down near Yosemite.' His voice was flat.

The lights of Calistoga came into sight. I noticed that Holly had stopped mauling her husband. I hadn't credited her with a great deal of sensitivity but I could now see that I was wrong. She knew he didn't like talking this way and I knew I had no business asking him questions. It had nothing to do with me but for a while it had stopped me thinking too much about what Victoria was doing.

'Don't talk to Sam about her,' Cliff said to me. 'He won't have her mentioned. He still has everything she owned, her clothes, her jewellery, all her possessions. He keeps her car in perfect condition, but no one drives it. It just sits there in the garage with a sheet over it when it isn't being maintained.'

'The white Jaguar?'

'You've seen it?'

'Yes.' That accounted for Sam Monahan's brusque dismissal of my enquiry about the E-Type but he had sounded angry, not grief-stricken. 'When did she die?'

'Twelve years ago.'

We were outside the hotel in Calistoga's main street now but there was no sign of the Chevrolet. I asked Cliff to drop me off outside the Sheriff's office.

'You'll come and see us filming again, won't you?' Holly said as I climbed out.

'I'll see,' I said.

'Your friend too, of course,' she added slyly.

'Her too,' I agreed. I had seen no point in telling them about my worries. Cliff certainly couldn't have driven any faster whatever I'd told him.

As I waved them off, Holly was back in her husband's lap again. He'd certainly married a handful of trouble but that was his problem, not mine. Mine was trouble enough.

Deputy Collis was writing a report in a glass-walled room at the back of the main office building. No one else was around and I walked through in response to his gesture.

I told him my problem.

'That's young Jimmy Paine,' he said, identifying the motor cycle officer without any need for head-scratching. He eyed me thoughtfully for a moment, obviously contemplating telling me something and then changing his mind. 'He's okay. Maybe over-enthusiastic at times, but, then, we're all that way when we begin.'

'He wouldn't do anything to harm Victoria?'

Collis frowned, fingering his heavy moustache. 'No,' he said but he didn't convince me because he wasn't convinced himself.

'Look, Collis, I don't want to push this but I must find Victoria and I don't much care if I have to rap some knuckles. You already owe me a little help.'

He scowled an enquiry.

'By talking too much to Sam Morahan.

You had no damn right telling him who Victoria is or who I am for that matter. Police business isn't supposed to be talked about to just anybody.'

He had turned dark red. 'Sam Monahan isn't just anybody. He's a big man around here and he cooperates with the police and helps out when he can. If we need extra hands he's always the first to offer his men.'

'All armed to the teeth and loaded for bear.'

'Don't leap to conclusions. Sam's a good guy. A few more citizens like him and we wouldn't have the kind of trouble we have in our cities today.'

I didn't argue with him. I didn't agree, but it wasn't my patch. If I'd had a man with an armoury like Monahan's near me I would have had fences keeping him in and burglars out, and I certainly wouldn't want him and his hired hands weighing in on any of my cases, however well-intentioned they might be.

'Give me a description of the car Lieutenant Bercovici is driving,' Collis said.

I described the car and gave him the licence number and waited while he put out a bulletin.

'Look, Mr Mace, there's something I should maybe tell you,' he said when he was through with the radio. He was still pink and I guessed that he was embarrassed at having been confronted with his loose talk. 'I don't see how it can have any connection but, well, like you I don't hold with coincidences. Jimmy Paine is Karen Raskin's brother.'

I thought hard about that for a while. I couldn't make a connection. Paine was young, early twenties maybe, and was unlikely to have any hang-ups about his late brother-in-law.

The telephone rang, sharp and jarring. Collis picked it up, spoke, listened, then handed it to me with a big grin under his moustache. 'She's okay,' he said.

'Victoria?' I said into the phone.

'Sorry I had to go but I couldn't find you.'

'That's okay. Where are you?'

'I'm with Karen Raskin. I think you should come over here.'

'I'm on my way,' I said.

I told Collis where she was and asked how to get there. The house lay about halfway between Calistoga and St Helena and he offered me the use of his own car. 'I'll follow on as soon as one of the guys comes in for a break.' He eyed me thoughtfully. 'She say why she wants you out there?'

'No.'

'Or anything about Jimmy Paine?'

'No.'

He nodded slowly. 'Maybe it is just a coincidence. I guess there have to be some once in a while.'

I took the keys to his car and headed for the door. 'Maybe,' I said, but I didn't believe it any more than he did.

14

I found the house with only one wrong turning along the way. It was a small, wood-structured building, with once-white clapboarded sides and front The roof hung low and a verandah stretched right across the front with steps up to the door. In the lights from Collis's car it didn't look to be in very good shape, but neither was it on the point of collapse.

Victoria let me into the house and if I held her too tightly for a moment she didn't complain.

Inside, the house showed signs of seldom having money spent on it. The furnishings were cheap and shabby and while the place was clean there was little to show much care and attention was lavished upon it.

'What happened to Jimmy Paine?' I asked.

'Who?'

'The young cop.'

'He was talking with Gary, the director, and he suddenly became anxious to leave. Gary had told him that we were around and who we are.'

'I'm sorry I wasn't there,' I said.

She looked deep into my eyes. 'Holly?' I nodded. 'Just talking. Honest.'

She smiled. 'This time I'll believe you. Next time . . . '

'What happened, anyway?'

'I followed him; Paine, you called him?'

'Yes.'

'We were back in Calistoga before I got around to asking myself why I was trailing him, after all he could have simply been worried that senior police officers were present when he was supposed to be on duty. Then I lost him, realised I was close to this house and decided to call and see if Karen would talk to me.'

'Paine's her brother,' I told her.

'I didn't know that.' She frowned, thinking, but like me she couldn't see a connection and shrugged the fact aside.

Opening the door into a tiny, well-lighted kitchen, Victoria introduced me to a small, dark-haired woman who was sitting at the table, hands clasped around a mug of coffee. Victoria had told me that ten years ago they had worn their hair alike. They certainly didn't do so now. Karen Raskin's dark hair was streaked with grey and hadn't been touched by a professional hand for years. Cropped short, it was pushed back from a face well set in angry lines. I couldn't see what appealed so much to Gil Raskin but, then, despite what the glossy magazines would have us believe, not many man-woman relationships are very well-designed.

'Karen has been telling me about Peter,' Victoria said. 'He was worried the night we . . . the police came. He'd been edgy for days.'

Karen nodded slowly. 'Peter never talked much. He thought a lot, though.'

'What was worrying him?' I asked.

'Like I said, he didn't talk much. I thought it was to do with his work at the Social Security office. He didn't like it, you know.' She stared unseeingly around the room. 'He only took the job because I didn't like him working in 'Frisco.'

'We talked with Gil,' I said.

Karen's head came up with a jerk, then sank again. 'I expect almost everyone knows about us, but I don't like to . . . ' Her voice trailed off and she stared at the dregs of her coffee as if hoping for an omen. 'We meet in a cabin at Vidal. It's a place we can be alone and where . . . there's nothing to remind us of Peter.'

Gil had told us he wanted to take her away from here so she didn't have grounds for complaint.

Karen stood up and took her coffee mug to the sink where she washed it out, her movements quick and angry.

'Gil doesn't think his brother had been to a psychiatrist. What do you think?'

'If he wanted to he would, he wouldn't ask me about it.'

'You didn't discuss things like that?' Victoria asked.

'No, they're, well, personal things, aren't they?'

I looked at Victoria and shrugged. I couldn't guess what kind of a marriage Peter and Karen Raskin had had but it certainly hadn't been one in which minds met.

'Earlier, you said something about a girl,' Victoria said, her voice gentle.

Karen was still at the sink, her back to us and now her shoulders stiffened. The silence dragged on. Outside, night birds called insults at one another and what could have been a cat rattled about in a trash can by the kitchen door.

'There wasn't anything to it,' Karen said, her voice louder than was needed.

'To what?'

'People like to talk, to make trouble.' She turned to face us, her chin up for the first time. There was a defiant gleam in her eyes which were a light hazel. For the first time I could see an attractive woman beneath the shell of dullness that had settled on her over the years. 'They said Peter was having an affair with a woman he worked with but he wasn't, I know it.'

'Who was she?'

'She didn't exist, I tell you.' There was silence for a moment, then Karen's shoulders sagged. 'She worked with him in St Helena.'

'What was her name?'

'Fran Morrisey, but I heard she was married a few years back. I don't know her name now.'

I waited but Victoria didn't seem to have any more questions.

'Where does your brother Jimmy live?' I asked.

'In St Helena.'

'Does he know about you and Gil?'

Karen nodded. 'Jimmy likes Gil. He's always saying I should marry him. He tries his best to stop people from finding out about us.'

Even to the extent of diverting customers from Bill Haigh's filling station it seemed.

'Can we talk again sometime?' Victoria asked.

Karen nodded. 'If you think it will help. You know, Peter couldn't have killed all those women. They never should have shot him.'

Victoria looked at her, then at me and I could tell that any moment now she would be confessing all. I didn't think it a very smart idea. Karen Raskin didn't strike me as being the most stable of people, even if she was a beaten-down version of what she might have been ten years ago. For all I knew she could have a shotgun within reach and I didn't fancy having to fight her for it. 'We'll come back another time, then,' I said hastily and pulled Victoria with me out through the kitchen door and onto the back porch.

'Wait, I'll get the light,' Karen said.

'This is no time for confessions,' I said to Victoria in the seconds before the lights snapped on.

'Okay, okay, I've got the message.'

The crack of a revolver and the thud as a bullet slammed into the wooden side of the house were almost simultaneous. I had grabbed Victoria and was diving for the darkness beyond the edge of the porch before conscious thoughts registered.

This must have been like a re-run of a nightmarish film for Victoria. Somewhere close to this point gunfire had erupted ten years ago, resulting in the death of her colleague and only ending when she had riddled Peter Raskin's body with bullets.

Another shot came, and inside the house Karen Raskin screamed. A nightmare was being played over again for her too.

I fumbled for the Smith & Wesson I had taken from Sam Monahan's collection and pushed Victoria into a dark shadowed space beneath the porch. 'Stay there,' I told her.

The shots had come from somewhere down towards the bottom of the plot of land on which the Raskin house stood. There were dark shapes of what looked like shrubs or small trees and a glimmer of light shining from the house touched on a broken-down shed. I headed towards the shed, zig-zagging according to the manual and hoping that whoever was doing the shooting hadn't read the same book.

A third shot whistled uncomfortably close to my head as I ran and I took a snap-shot. There was a satisfying boom and my bullet ricocheted off the roof of the shed. Judging from the clatter the shed was made from corrugated sheeting.

I could hear shouts and somewhere, far

off, a baby was crying. Dogs barked and over it all I heard a car approaching. The headlights swung across the open space between me and the trees and I threw myself sideways as the lights hit me. It was a smart move because another shot zipped through the space I had just vacated.

Then there was another shot, this time from a different place and I couldn't tell where it was aimed. The car had stopped and I heard a voice yelling loud: 'This is the police.' I recognised Deputy Collis.

By now I had reached the trees and was maybe ten paces from the shed.

'Freeze!' Collis's voice came again, yelling.

I turned my head and made out a black shape running towards the house The shape didn't slow down and I snapped off a hopeful shot. So too did Collis. From the echoing boom of his gun he was using something that would have halted one of Hannibal's pack-animals. The running black shape continued moving but its direction had changed and so too had its form of propulsion. Instead of leg power taking it towards the house, it was whirling sideways, clear of the ground but only for a moment. It hit dirt and in the beam of Collis's headlamps I could see a slight, dark-clad figure, parts of which reflected the light.

I ran towards the figure, and Collis was coming too. When we reached the body Victoria had emerged from where I had left her. The three of us gathered around the still form, all with guns out and all tense with the unavoidable excitement of the moment.

It was quieter now. Even the dogs had stopped barking. But the baby still howled.

'Thanks,' I said to Collis. 'You came in there like the 7th Cavalry.'

'It's no goddamn joke, Mace,' he said quietly.

'I'm not joking, Sheriff.'

The kitchen door of the Raskin house banged open and I looked up to see Karen standing there, staring down at us.

Collis nudged the body with a foot and turned it over. There was a hole in his chest from which blood still oozed.

'Oh, Christ, Mace,' Victoria said softly.

I hadn't heard Karen Raskin come down from the porch to where we stood but suddenly she was standing with us and starting up a moan which came from deep down inside her body.

Then Deputy Sheriff Collis was glaring at me, his flashlamp in my eyes. 'What the hell is this, Mace? What for God's sake is going on here?'

I didn't know.

I didn't know why we'd been shot at, even if I did know why I had started shooting back.

Top of the list of things I didn't know was why, of all people, Jimmy Paine, the young motor-cycle cop, should have taken it into his head to open fire on us.

About the only thing I did know was that Jimmy Paine was decidedly dead.

15

However different they might be in detail, cops everywhere have a lot in common with one another. Kill a policeman in Liverpool, London, Paris, Los Angeles, or Outer Baluchistan, and all hell breaks loose. Calistoga was no exception except that, given the reduced man-power, it was a fairly subdued kind of hell.

Central to it all, of course was J. D. Collis. There was no doubt that his shot had killed Jimmy Paine. There were no other wounds; just one in the side of his chest big enough to take a clenched fist. Collis went through a rapid string of emotional responses: anger, which began it, eventually running down to a kind of sullen remorse. At no time did he put into words what must have been in his mind. However it would all eventually add up, he knew that Jimmy Paine's death was a result of Victoria and me deciding to come to Calistoga for our reunion.

Victoria wanted to call her boss in LA and request an official reinvestigation of the killings of ten years ago. If she could convince him there was a connection he would have the authority if only because one of his men, Gerry Mandan, had been killed. How such authority would sit with the local law enforcement officers was another matter.

'Okay, do that,' I agreed. 'But there's something else we need to talk about.'

'What's that?' We were parking the car outside the Mount View now. 'And don't tell me your mind's on sex again because I'm not in the mood.'

'I think I'm about to put you even less in the mood.'

'Why, now what's happened?'

'I think Jimmy Paine was shot by mistake tonight. Those first shots, three of them, came from over near the old shed. I fired in that direction, another one came back at me. Then there was a fifth shot only this time it was from further over towards the trees. Now, I don't know if it was Paine starting at the shed and running away but if it was, why did he turn round and run towards the house which is where he was headed when Collis shot him?'

'You think there were two people?'

I opened the car door and climbed out. The night air felt cold and I shivered. 'Yes, I do. Maybe they were working together but I doubt it. My guess is that Jimmy was watching the house, maybe thinking he would protect his sister if we were too tough with her. When the shooting started he waited to see who was shooting at whom and then joined in. I reckon that, like me, he was firing at whoever was at the shed. Then he decided to go to his sister and Collis hit him with a lucky shot.'

Victoria was out of the car now and I put an arm around her shoulders. She was cold too. We went inside, collected the room key from the old man on duty and went upstairs.

Later, warm again in bed, Victoria changed her mind about sex and we made love gently and without any of the animal passion that had gripped us down by the lakeshore. It was no less enjoyable;

there was a warm, knowing intimacy that we hadn't shared before.

There was no reason why, in the morning, I should feel rested but I did. While I showered, shaved, and sorted out clean clothes from a diminishing pile, Victoria called her boss in the LAPD. I heard only snippets from her end of the conversation and it was clear that she had some initial reluctance to overcome. Eventually, however, she won him over and he agreed to send up files and all the original case notes from both her report and that of Gerry Mandan. He also promised to put in a call to the County Sheriff and make a formal request for his cooperation. Victoria planned to talk personally to Collis and ask him very nicely to play along. That was only a polite formality once she had official backing, but it was the best course.

This morning she dressed in blue, mostly dark, and was slightly formal-looking in a calf-length skirt and matching tailored jacket. She looked marginally more like a cop but she certainly didn't look unfeminine. If I had been Deputy Collis I would have been impressed, but maybe I was prejudiced. I helped her tie a black scarf which, set against a light-blue high-collared blouse, rounded out the uniform-like look. I kissed the tip of her nose so as not to disturb her make-up or my hormones, then we went downstairs, picked up an envelope Sam Monahan had sent over and crossed the street for breakfast.

'I think I should see Collis on my own,' she told me over coffee.

'Okay, but from here on I think we should have a house rule. Don't go anywhere you can be shot at by our unknown friend unless you have company. And choose your company carefully; remember we have no idea who he is. All we do know is that indoors, out in the open, night or day, he'll have a go.'

'I know, you don't need to remind me.'

'How long do you expect to be with Collis?'

'Once he's cooperating, I want to review all their case notes from ten years ago. I would guess a day, maybe two.'

I told her I would call in and see Ruth

Beckerman. 'I'll take up her invitation to have us to dinner, and ask her a few more questions about the Raskin family. If she hasn't the answers off the top of her head she can dig them out between now and whenever we sit down to eat.'

'Talking mass-murder over dinner doesn't sound like a whole lot of fun,' Victoria said, echoing the remark the lady in the bookshop had made.

I escorted Victoria along the street to the Sheriff's office, then went up to see Ruth Beckerman. A different young woman sat in the chair facing the head of the stairs. She was alone, bored, pretty in a small-town way and, judging from the cover of the paperback she was reading, didn't have the same devoted interest Jane Cole had shown in Ruth Beckerman's work.

'They're both in San Francisco,' she told me. 'There's a conference and they wanted to hear some of the speeches.' She made such a desire sound roughly akin to deliberately pouring itching powder down the inside of a plaster cast on a broken leg. 'They'll be back tomorrow evening.'

She laid down the paperback and looked up at me through dark lashes. 'Anything I can do for you?'

I had the feeling that if I'd taken her up on her thinly veiled suggestion she would have run screaming down the stairs before I'd unbuttoned my first innuendo. 'Thanks, but I'll wait until they're back.'

She shrugged, pouting in what she probably thought was a provocative manner. I went down the stairs and into the heat of the morning sunshine. On the street I opened up Sam Monahan's envelope. There were three names, complete with descriptions. One matched the yellow-haired man, the others could have been his two companions on the day of the hijack but I couldn't see the principal negotiators also handling their own dirty work. With each name was an address and a further address was clearly their business front. All were in San Francisco. Eddie's man appeared to have done a good job. I hoped his ears were still attached to his head.

I wandered into the bookshop which was just opening up for the day. The young blonde recognised me and smiled and I began guiltily looking for something to buy when all I was really doing was killing time. A selection of books on San Francisco caught my eye and I pulled one down and began leafing through it as a line of thought developed.

Sam Monahan's threats came from an outfit based in San Francisco, Gil Raskin had said his brother had left a job in the city to move out here when he married Karen, and Cliff Monahan had said he'd owned a club there. None of these items was necessarily related but as I had nothing else to do and I had promised Sam I would take an interest in his troubles I decided on a little trip.

I bought a street map on the city from the blonde lady, thus mildly salving my conscience, went back to the Sheriff's office to tell Victoria where I was going, noted that Collis was finding it easier to work closely with her than I liked, and drove out of town before I changed my mind.

The day I'd arrived I had driven south from the airport in San Francisco, crossed the San Mateo Bridge and swung up around Oakland, past Concord and north to Calistoga. As a result I'd seen nothing of the city because the heart of the place, apart from being fog-shrouded that day, lies north of the airport.

This time, I went down to Vallejo, then Richmond, and detoured across the bridge to San Rafael; all so that I could enter the city across the Golden Gate Bridge.

Mist clung low over the harbour waters but I could make out the dim shape of Alcatraz and, poking up into the sun-shine, the tips of various high-rise buildings, among them the unmistakeable shape of the Transamerica Pyramid.

Once in the city, with my new street map wedged across the steering wheel, I rolled up the hills south of the harbour.

The address Sam Monahan had given me for his would-be associates turned out to be a building big enough to feature in the credit title sequences of one of those movies that threaten to bare all about intrigue in big business but which all too often bare only the leading lady's best features.

The company had offices on the twentieth floor and I went up in one of those external glass-sided elevators designed to send any sufferer from vertigo over the edge in ten seconds flat. I wasn't a sufferer but I wouldn't have liked making the journey with a hangover.

Occidental Investments Inc., had a single office suite which in these surroundings meant four rooms any one of which could have housed a Saturday afternoon's crowd at Tranmere Rovers when they were still a league side. The first one was occupied by a version of the young woman I'd seen a couple of hours earlier at Ruth Beckerman's office. She had a big city sheen over her small-town prettiness but that was about the only difference. She was even reading a paperback, only hers was one of those thick bestsellers which differ from less popular books only in that two words are used where one is enough.

One of the names Sam had given me was Koven and I asked if he was in today, trying to think of something to say to him if he was.

'He's out,' she said, then waved a hand which knew more about manicures than typing towards the door into the adjoining room. 'Mr Markowitz is in; he knows all Mr Koven's business.'

Markowitz was another of the names Sam Monahan had given me so it was worth talking to him. Except that I was probably wasting my time here anyway. This kind of operation was likely to be way over my head. The girl took her long fingernails and swaying hips through the door while I wondered where I should start the improvisation needed to extract some kind of information from Markowitz.

When the girl came back to wordlessly indicate I should squeeze past her through the doorway into the next room I wasn't very far ahead.

A man was sitting behind a desk long enough to comfortably accommodate the girl with the fingernails. I recognised him. His yellow hair was straggly and his face pale enough to serve as the before half of a suntan oil ad. Despite its colour the face was hard and humourless, the kind you try not to argue with. I didn't think he would recognise me, I'd been behind the windscreen when I wasn't behind the rocks. I certainly hoped he wouldn't, especially if he was carrying the gun he'd used to crease Sam's Chevy.

He didn't stand up, smile, or give any indication that I was welcome. More importantly, there was no flicker of recognition. I didn't tell him my name, deciding that he was the type who probably went through life neither giving nor receiving such small courtesies and settled for telling him that I was an associate of Sam Monahan's and had a proposition to make. I tried to make it sound like one of those offers people like him can't refuse but there are some things that do not sound right if the accent is wrong.

'What kind of proposition?' he asked, noticeably unimpressed.

'I'm inside,' I said. 'You can use a man like me.'

He thought about that for a while but thinking wasn't a strong point and he soon looked like a man with an incipient headache. He couldn't be as important as Sam thought.

'Why not call Mr Koven and ask him?' I suggested.

He glanced at the wall to my right. A row of clocks gave the time all around the world. 'He's out of town until tomorrow night.'

'Okay,' I said. 'Call him later and tell him I want to deal. I can give him Monahan's business without any hassles and maybe leads into damn near every winery in Napa County.'

'Where can we reach you?'

'I'll call,' I said. 'At the weekend.'

'What's your name?'

'Osterman,' I said, having decided he didn't seem to be the literary type.

I left him to it, went out past the girl who was reading her paperback with the aid of a fingernail which traced the words. So far as I could see she wasn't moving her lips so perhaps I hadn't given her enough credit.

The office building was on Sutter Street and coming down in the elevator I studied the view which was impressive. The air was clear up here and even the touch of mist lying over the bay wasn't enough to conceal the bridges and the islands. Occidental Investment's offices had looked the opposite way, probably because the attractions of a view of the Golden Gate Bridge was outweighed by also having to stare at Alcatraz all day. That was liable to lead to sleepless nights even if it was merely a tourist lure nowadays.

I took my thoughts into Sam Monahan's Chevrolet and once more studied the names and private addresses he had sent over. I decided that Markowiz and Koven were the two I should concentrate upon. I knew where they were; the other might be spending the day at home and would not welcome visitors.

Koven's address was way over to the west and I was busily negotiating Union Square when I spotted a tail I wasn't looking for one, but he had the misfortune to tangle with a midday drunk. The accompanying squeal of tyres attracted my attention and when he came up behind me two sets of traffic lights later I was sure.

I kept heading the same way, looking for a place to turn and lose him. I didn't have the chance. We were riding convoy through an area filled with Victorian era timber-clad houses. Any book on turn-of-the-century architecture would have been proud to have them on its cover and several probably did. Some of the side turnings had similarly constructed properties but time had taken its toll and a general air of seediness prevailed. I made the mistake of swinging into one of these side roads. I should have known better. Never try giving another driver the slip on his own turf; it's in the manual.

16

I knew I was in trouble when I turned the corner to find myself facing a crumbling brick wall. I could neither go on nor turn around. All I could do was back up and as I banged the Chevy into reverse the other car slid up close behind me. I watched the driver in my rear-view mirror; one-to-one he shouldn't prove too much trouble and if the worst happened I always had Sam Monahan's Smith & Wesson. One way and another I was becoming dependent upon the little wine-maker. Of course, if it hadn't been for him I wouldn't have been here anyway but I didn't let that discolour my opinions.

Then the passenger door of the pursuing car opened and someone clambered out. I hadn't seen anyone beside the driver and that wasn't surprising. He was a little man, no more than four feet tall, with a normal-sized head set at a stiffly awkward angle into thin misshapen shoulders. He didn't look too menacing but the gun in his hand did. It would have looked big in a giant's hand. In the dwarf's hand it seemed heavy enough to take out the San Francisco 49ers and Everton's first team squad put together.

Obviously I was outnumbered. I eased the revolver out of its clip and onto my lap, then pressed gently down on the door handle until I heard the catch release. I took a deep breath and went out low and fast.

I surprised the driver, a young dark-complexioned man with tightly curled black hair. He wasn't showing a gun but he was scrabbling at his shoulder as I straightened up. He saw the business end of my Smith & Wesson, took the hint, stopped moving and stared thoughtfully at my face.

'Tell your friend to drop the cannon before he gets muscle fatigue,' I said.

He flicked a sideways glance at the dwarf, then came back to me with a small smile touching his lips. He was young, good-looking, of Spanish-American ancestry, and didn't appear to give a damn. In fact he was enjoying this. I've met the type before; they can be dangerous. The usual rules of behaviour do not apply. 'He doesn't take orders from me,' he told me. 'In fact, there are not many people he does take orders from.'

I took him at his word and showed the little man the hole in the end of the revolver. 'Drop the gun,' I said. 'The alternative will have no appeal for you.'

The dwarf smiled with all the charm of a shark from the bay. The big automatic was pointing right at me. We had one of those situations which are best known as academic. Whoever pressed the trigger first stood a better than even chance of dying before his opponent hit the ground.

The dark-haired young man seemed to like the situation. 'This is what my old grandpappy would call a Mexican stand-off,' he remarked.

I agreed, so I turned the Smith & Wesson back to him. 'In that case, point out to your friend that it isn't me and him any more, it's me and you.'

He thought about this for a moment

and came to a conclusion. 'I think you should both put up your guns and we'll take this up another time.'

A glance at the dwarf told me that he didn't like it but was reluctantly coming to the same conclusion. Whatever their instructions, killing me was not on the schedule.

We had both let our guns point to the ground and were thinking of ways and means of neutralising the situation to the point where it was safe to get back into our cars when the dark-haired man took control.

Having already decided he was dangerous I should never have taken my eyes off him, but I did. He came at me too fast for me to do anything but try to minimise the power with which his shoulder hit me in the middle. I dropped the gun, tried a grab for it, then changed my mind and brought up a punch from the far end of desperation. It connected, not fully but enough to slow him down. Then the little man sneaked in under our bodies and kicked my gun out of reach. The young guy hit me hard along the side of the jaw and would have made a mess of my nose if I hadn't seen it coming. I clasped my hands together and swung a hard blow at his stomach. The breath rushed out of him and he began doubling over. Before he was too far down I brought my still clasped hands up and hit him in the soft flesh under the chin. His head went back with a click and he crashed over backwards.

I spun around ready for the little man but he had scurried back far enough to be out of reach and was showing me the big gun again. 'Go ahead,' I told him. 'He told me you don't like taking orders. What did Markowitz tell you? Rough me up but don't kill me? Okay, so kill me, then explain it all to Koven.'

A dull light glimmered at the back of his eyes. Tough as he thought he was, Koven carried weight which is what I had hoped.

I saw my gun a few paces away and moved towards it. The dwarf made a noise at the back of his throat. 'Don't be silly,' I said. 'The party's over.'

I picked up my gun, put it away, then

helped the young man to his feet. He was recovering fast; another five minutes and he would be ready for round two. I pushed him into the driver's seat of the other car, in the process relieving him of his revolver.

I tried to think of some suitable message to send to Markowitz but I couldn't. Walking into his office had been stupid and given it all to do over again I wouldn't have played it this way. Come to it, another time I wouldn't have agreed to tackle Sam Monahan's problem at all.

Back in my car I drove up onto the front of someone's untended garden and manoeuvred myself around the other vehicle. Winding down the window I handed the young man's gun to the dwarf. 'Tell him next time he pulls a gun on me I'll make him eat it. As for you, what I have in mind is somewhat different. If I were you, I'd start carrying a smaller weapon right away.'

He glared at me but Koven's absent presence was too strong for him to do anything other than look ugly, which he managed without too much difficulty.

I drove around a couple of corners looking for a street sign which gave me a clue where I was, then headed generally downhill working on the principle that this was the way to reach the harbour.

I found a place to park the car, then used the men's room at a sea-food restaurant to tidy myself up. Even if I had been in a rough house, at least I could face the waitress with the confidence of a man with nothing to declare out his appetite.

Later I checked a telephone book for the address of the AF of M Local, drove over there and tried vainly to pick up on the fact that Gil Raskin had referred to his brother as having been in the music business. For all I knew he could have been a piano-tuner or a sheet music salesman but I asked the lady in charge of records to see if they had anyone by that name on their books ten years ago and more. She couldn't help me because lapsed members' details were junked after only a couple of years.

'You wouldn't believe the number of people who come into, then drift out of this business. If we kept everyone's listing we'd need twice the floor space,' she told me.

I believed her and left and on the way out noticed a poster which told me that Monty Budwig was playing tonight with a somewhat more promising collection of musicians than those assembled at Sam Monahan's party.

I took the opportunity of being in San Francisco to take a look at a few of the tourist sights, then went into a hotel and used a payphone to call Collis. He told me that Victoria was right beside him. He made it sound very cosy. I waited until she came on the line.

'What are you doing?' I asked. 'Sitting in his lap?'

She laughed and, after a moment, so did I. 'What's happened?' she asked.

'What makes you think anything's happened? Can't I just be jealous like any normal man?'

'I know you, remember.'

'I had a little trouble,' I acknowledged. 'But it sorted itself out. How's it going at your end?'

'Slowly, but we're getting through it. We're planning on working late here, then Jack's taking me home to dinner.'

'Jack?'

'That's what the J in J.D. Collis stands for.'

'Now listen to . . . '

'He tells me his wife makes the best four-way chili this side of the Rockies.'

'His wife?'

She laughed again. 'Right. And I might stay out there, it will save the drive back into town. Unless . . . '

I liked the thought of the 'unless but so far I hadn't justified my trip to the city. 'No, you stay there and keep safe. There's a couple of things I can do here tonight.'

'Okay.' There was a tiny pause. 'I miss you.'

'I'll see you in the morning,' I said. 'And tomorrow night we'll make up for tonight.'

'You can count on it,' she said.

The hotel I was calling from looked pricey and as I didn't have any baggage with me I went in search of somewhere cheaper and on the way picked up a shirt, a disposable razor pack, and a cheap shoulder bag emblazoned with the name of a firm manufacturing running shoes.

I took a room at the Holiday Inn, showered, shaved, put on the new shirt, and went out again. I killed a few hours taking in more tourist sights, then made my way up to Vallejo Street.

The Keystone Korner is located, appropriately enough, a few steps away from a police station but no Kops were around. I was early and the place was barely a quarter-full. I bought a beer, told the bartender I was a friend of Monty Budwig's, which was stretching our fleeting acquaintance, and settled down to wait.

When Monty came in he was pleased to see me again but showed no surprise when I said I wanted to ask him some questions.

'I was talking to Bill Berry earlier,' he said. 'He told me you're a cop. He also said I shouldn't hold it against you and that you're okay.'

That made it easier. 'I'm trying to dig up background on someone,' I said. 'The trouble is, he's been dead ten years and the trail is colder than he is.'

'How do I come in?'

'You don't, except that he was connected with the music business here in San Francisco.' I told him Peter Raskin's name which rang no bells but Monty said he'd ask around. We had a drink together, talked some and then it was time for the first set.

The music was good and as I had taken the precaution of walking up here I didn't have to worry about drinking over the limit.

At the end of the first set Monty came back to the bar with the drummer from the band. 'Freddie knows your man,' Monty told me.

'Sure, he was mixed up in all those killings, right?'

'That's the one.'

'I never would have thought it,' Freddie said. 'Pete was such a quiet guy. Just came in, played his set, and went home again. Then one night he didn't show and I heard he'd quit the business.'

'He was a musician?'

'Yes, a piano player. He was the house pianist at the Half Note on Powell and Washington.'

'Thanks very much,' I said. I checked the time. 'Maybe I could find someone there now who remembers him.'

'You won't,' Freddie said. 'It folded years ago.'

The glow of a possible lead faded. 'Anything else you can tell me?' I asked.

Freddie thought for a while, then shook his head slowly. 'Sorry.'

'Ah, well, have a drink,' I said and called the bartender.

We talked of various things, mostly musical. Somewhere along the way Monty began recounting the problems he'd had with the young musicians he'd taken up to Laronne.

That was when Freddie suddenly straightened up and snapped his fingers. 'Hey, I just remembered, the guy who owned the Half Note has some connection with that outfit. He'll know more about Pete Raskin than anyone.'

'What's his name?' I asked but something was starting to tell me.

'Cliff Monahan,' Freddie said. 'Isn't his old man the owner of the whole goddamn county?'

'Something like that,' I said.

The patrons in the Korner were growing restive and Monty and Freddie finished off their drinks and went back to their instruments.

I didn't pay as much attention to the second set as the music and musicians deserved. I was too busy trying to see how I could fit today's events and information into what I'd known before I drove into the city. I couldn't.

Later, I walked back down to my hotel, hoping that by morning everything would be clearer.

I took a wrong turning and found myself down on Fisherman's Wharf so I cut through an open courtyard lined with small stores and dotted with flowering trees.

Two other people were using the same way; both were slim and slightly built and the way their arms were wrapped around one another told me they were anxious to get back to someplace that was even more secluded than this. I had soft soles to my shoes and wasn't making any noise so they didn't know I was there. They stopped walking, faced one another and kissed long enough to damage the oxygenation of their blood. I stopped too and stared into a store window feeling mildly curious because I was close enough now to see that they were both women.

When they moved off again I did too. At that moment they turned to go out of the courtyard and the light from the windows of the Howard Johnson hotel fell fully on their faces. I recognised them. One was Ruth Beckerman, the psychiatrist who was such a good friend of Sam Monahan's; the other was Jane Cole, her young assistant.

After they had gone from my sight I waited a few minutes before I followed. Whatever relationship they had didn't concern me. It wasn't illegal here, nor in my country, and I didn't find it at all distasteful the way some people do. But it did interest me that so many of the people I had met since I'd arrived three days ago should turn out to have secret selves they kept hidden from public gaze.

Somewhere, among all these secrets, was the one that most concerned me. If everyone had been what they seemed, it would have been easy to uncover. The way things were developing, finding one secret among so many would make needle-searching in haystacks a breeze.

17

I didn't sleep too well that night. Maybe it was through trying to think too much, maybe it was my digestion which was suffering from too much drinking at Keystone Korner, maybe it was because Victoria wasn't beside me. Whatever or whomever, by morning I felt and looked like an extra for a crowd scene in *The Hunchback of Notre Dame*. Thanks to lying half in and half out of the bed during the couple of hours' sleep I did get, I could have played the lead without padding in the back of my jacket.

I checked out of the hotel, risked a cup of coffee, then pointed the car towards Koven's house intent on picking up where I had left off yesterday when the dwarf and his Mexican companion had stepped into my life.

The house was neither as big nor as impressive as I expected for a top man in the Organisation. Maybe they were on short-time working, maybe they'd been told to keep a low public profile, maybe I'd seen too many movies. Or maybe all was not what I'd been led to believe.

I parked the car around the corner, walked quickly past the front of the house, then went down a side alley, hopped over a fence very quickly before I had time to change my mind and burgled my way into Koven's home. Inside were all the necessities of modern living; microwave cooker and ice-box complete with ice cube maker in the kitchen; video recorder, giant-screen TV, water-bed, and in the bathroom, gold-plated taps. Somehow, the fact there was a dusty, malodorous air about the place and that all the electronic goodies were crammed in tiny rooms and forced to share space with furnishings that any self-respecting junk dealer would have handed over to famine relief long ago reinforced my sneaking feeling that Koven was somewhat less important than the flash offices on Sutter Street had suggested.

I made a quick but thorough check on contents of drawers and cupboards and came up empty. Koven kept no files, letters or books, in fact the only piece of paper with writing on it was a calendar beside the telephone which had a few numbers scrawled on it in pencil.

One number was out of town and I tried that first. A girl's voice answered, telling me that I was calling the Laronne Winery and asking how she could help me. I hung up without speaking and tried the first of the local numbers, the only one of three without a name alongside it. Another girl told me that this was Occidental Investments Inc., and thanked me for calling. I hung up on this one too, letting her return to her paperback and manicure.

One of the remaining numbers was marked 'Lew', the other 'Carlos'. I tried Lew and drew no reply. Carlos answered halfway through the first ring. Putting on my best American accent, I told him that this was his lucky day and he had won an opportunity to share with a select few the benefits of the Gastronome's Book Club. He started to tell me what I could do, using some choice words and allowing me to be fairly certain I was talking to the handsome heavy who had trailed me yesterday. Abruptly, he stopped speaking. Maybe my accent was not as good as I thought. For a moment we listened to one another breathing, then he hung up.

I left Koven's house and drove across town to the office building. I was edging my car between a pair of executive limousines which belonged to one of the many, doubtless genuine, companies occupying the building, when I saw Carlos and the girl with the fingernails hurrying from the main entrance and scrambling into a car. I couldn't see the dwarf, who by now I guessed was named Lew; but, then, I hadn't seen him yesterday either. For all I knew he was taking a nap in the ashtray.

I tossed a metal coin, which came down heads. I stayed where I was until the car was out of sight, then went into the building and found a red-faced uniformed individual and persuaded him to risk his immortal soul by exchanging confidential information for a ten dollar bill. My guesses were coming right.

Occidental Investments Inc. had been in residence for less than a month, they never had any callers, and if I wanted his opinion they knew as much about investment counselling as he did about the reproductive cycle of the golden hamster. I left the porter fondling his ten-spot and went up in the external elevator on what I was fairly certain was a wasted journey.

I was right; the offices were deserted and had been vacated so fast the door wasn't even closed let alone locked. Ten minutes showed me there was even less paperwork here than at Koven's house. Even the girl's paperback was missing.

I was standing in the middle of the biggest of the offices when I heard someone come in from the corridor and a man's voice calling for Gloria.

I put a hand under my jacket so that I could feel the reassurance of the Smith & Wesson and went out to meet him. He was short, overweight, sweaty, and looked as if he had slept in his suit.

'Who the hell are you?' he asked. Then,

edging towards the door he called, 'Lew, Carlos, Marco,' in a tentative way.

I showed him the gun and he stopped moving. I went closer to him, pressed the muzzle of the revolver two inches into his midriff and relieved him of his wallet. His driver's licence told me he was Richard M. Koven. 'I think we should sit down and talk, Mr Koven.' He did as I suggested. 'I was told you were out of town until tonight.'

'I changed my . . . hey, how in hell do you know . . . ' He stopped speaking and we looked at one another.

'I talked to Markowitz, and I've also met Gloria, Carlos and Little Lew. Is that the whole team or have you any other midgets hiding under the rug?'

'Who are you?'

I thought about that for a while, then decided to tell him a story which might well sound true to what I suspected was the well-tuned ear of a small-time conman.

'You have been using our name in vain, Mr Koven. You let Sam Monahan think he was dealing with us, when all he was doing was playing the pigeon to a team of little-league players who really should know better.'

'It wasn't my idea, believe me.'

I doubted he had much acquaintance with honesty but I suspected this much might be the truth. He didn't show any overt signs of brainpower and if his lifestyle was truly reflected by his home he was also singularly lacking in sophistication. 'Then whose idea was it?'

'I don't know.'

I put the muzzle of the Smith & Wesson against his right eye. He squeezed the eye and its companion tight shut.

'I don't, I swear to God I don't. The instructions came in the mail. We just followed orders.'

'What did you hope to get out of it?'

'We were on twenty-five thousand each for the four of us. And expenses while we played Monahan along.'

'The four being you, Markowitz, Carlos and Lew?'

'That's right.'

'What are their last names, Carlos and Lew?'

'Carlos Rivera and Lew Santini.'

'What about Gloria?'

'She's Carlos's girl.'

'These letters with your instructions, let me see them.'

'They're gone, I had to burn them as soon as they were read.'

'Where were they postmarked?'

'Different places, here in town, one time Sacramento, never twice the same.'

So he had looked. That sounded convincing, a man like Koven would always be watching out for an edge.

'What did you have to do?'

He opened his eyes. 'Hijack a few trucks, damage some consignments, just keep Monahan on the hop until he was softened up for the big one.'

'And what was that to be?'

'I don't know.' My disbelief must have shown. 'Some big operation. We had to make Monahan think he wouldn't be allowed to refuse the offer when it was made.'

'What did your last set of instructions tell you?'

Koven's face changed. 'Oh, Jesus.

Markowitz will be on his way.'

'To do what?'

'I don't know. He'll get his orders when he reaches town.'

'Where?'

'The Mount View Hotel in Calistoga.'

Well, well, well. Couldn't be closer, I thought. Then it occurred to me that having the yellow-haired man under the same roof as Victoria was not very nice.

'What time does he arrive?'

'Sometime this afternoon.'

I thought about it all for a few moments. 'Okay,' I said eventually, taking the gun far enough away from him so that he could concentrate. 'This is what we'll do.'

It took a while and several telephone calls to set Koven's cronies on the way to Los Angeles where they would be out of my hair and within reach of Victoria's colleagues in the LAPD. I didn't expect to be thanked; sending criminals to LA beats shipping coal to Newcastle or the unemployed to Liverpool.

Then I spent a few minutes convincing Koven that if he played the game to my rules he would end up on the best team in the league. I risked laying it on thickly, working on the principle that con artists are the biggest potential pigeons in the world if only because they are psychologically incapable of believing anyone is smarter and more devious than they are themselves.

When I left him in his suite of four offices, still sweaty and in need of sleep, I was reasonably certain he was neutralised for a while. What he would do if he discovered what happened next was another matter. Also, another matter was what might happen if the Organisation discovered that not only had Koven and his team pretended to have connections with them, but I had committed the same sin myself.

From the lobby of the office block I used the porter's telephone to call Victoria. She promised not to return to the Mount View until I was back in town and to have one of Collis's men put on surveillance of Markowitz. It was important to know who, if anyone, contacted him. She also agreed to call her boss in

LA and have Carlos, Gloria and Lew picked up at the airport when they flew in tonight. I decided against asking the police to watch Koven because he would frighten easily and I didn't know how carefully they would handle it, especially as there wasn't too much I wanted them to know.

'What time will you be back?' Victoria asked.

'I'm leaving right away but I want to make a stop in St Helena.'

'Don't be late.'

'Why, what have you in mind?' I asked, trying my best to achieve the physical impossibility of leering over the telephone.

'I need help with the goddamn paperwork,' she told me.

'Isn't Collis helping?'

'He's lost his glasses again. Conveniently.'

'Okay, I'll be there as soon as I can.'

'Why are you calling at St Helena?'

'To see a lady,' I said mysteriously and hung up before she could ask me any more questions. It wasn't that I wanted to keep secrets from Victoria; I didn't even know if it was worth keeping a secret, but until I had visited the Social Security office in St Helena I wanted to play this close to my chest.

18

Unlike my drive out to San Francisco, I took the shortest route back and bent the speed limit whenever I could. Sightseeing was no longer on my list of priorities.

The Social Security office in St Helena was not what I had expected. That was probably due to the image the words conjured up in a British mind. There were no drab green and cream painted walls or linoleum covered floors, neither were there those red plastic-covered seats which fill offices of the Welfare State in Britain. Here, the impression was of people who cared and people who mattered. It should have been that way in Britain too, but almost never was. Yet another impression or prejudice brought to America had bitten the dust in the face of reality. It almost never is like the movies. Sometimes that's a pity, other times it isn't.

I had skipped lunch and was feeling

slightly in need of food when I parked outside the office and went in to ask a hopeful question. Fate, for once, smiled on me.

Karen Raskin had admitted her husband's association with a young woman named Fran Morrisey who had later, she thought, married. Fran Morrisey, now named Fran Morrisey Hunt, still worked at the office and had no objection to talking about her old love affair.

'I don't think Petey did it,' she said when we had completed formalities and I was drinking coffee in her cramped but bright office. 'In those days I didn't understand much about men and I certainly didn't understand myself. That came later, after Petey and the baby and everything. I went away for a while, learned about myself, married Jeff Hunt, and came back here to help others gain freedom from their repressions.'

I stared at her over the edge of the paper cup of coffee. I had never read any of the books I now mentally associated her with, and if that was how people talked after reading them I never would.

'You had a baby?'

She shook her head, her light brown hair bouncing with unbottled vitality. 'I couldn't handle that kind of problem then, I was only eighteen. Petey insisted on an abortion and because he was so much older, and seemed to know how to handle such things I went along.'

'You knew he was married, of course.'

'Yes. I was impressionable. I thought married men were more attractive, more mature, you know, than boys my own age.'

'Why did you split with him?'

A tiny frown appeared on her brightly cheerful face. 'It was after the abortion. I was pretty low and I began wondering why I couldn't have his baby too. Of course, by then it was too late.'

'Who else had his babies?'

'His wife, of course.' She laughed. 'I couldn't see the difference in those days.'

I hadn't seen any sign of children at the Raskin house and no one had mentioned there were any. Then again, there was no reason why anyone should have told me. 'How many children did he have?'

'Two, a boy and a girl.'

'You saw them?'

'No, but he told me about them.'

I couldn't see any future down that particular alley. 'You said he couldn't have been responsible for the killings. What makes you think so?'

I expected a string of multi-syllabled words hacked out of some treatise or other on self-analysis. I'd misjudged her. 'Petey was kind and gentle, always making jokes. He wouldn't kill women, he liked them too much. I wasn't the only one he saw. There were others, mostly like me, young and unattached. But it wasn't just sexual conquests, the way it is with some men. He just enjoyed being around women and he was never cruel or crude. He was just, well, a nice man.'

It wouldn't have carried any weight in a court of law but she impressed me. 'Were you interviewed by the police?'

'No. By the time I heard he was suspected he was already dead. So I just went away.'

There was nothing else she could have done. 'Thanks,' I said.

'Why are you asking? It was all a long time ago.'

'I know. Maybe too long to be digging it all up again, but there's a reason.'

'And you can't tell me what the reason is.'

I smiled at her. 'That's right.'

I went out to the car, then changed my mind and walked down the street to buy a sandwich at the first diner I came to. I sat in a seat by the window watching the cars go by. The diner was equipped with a juke box with selection terminals in every booth. The music was mostly leisurely middle of the road material but I found a Count Basie record down at the bottom of the list and listened to 'Shiny Stockings' and thought about Peter and Karen Raskin.

Maybe it was natural for his wife and lover to think he was innocent of the murders; but for no good reason I could put a finger on, I was beginning to side with Karen Raskin and Fran Morrisey Hunt.

On the way back to the car I came to a payphone and called Victoria at the

Sheriff's office in Calistoga. She almost burned with curiosity but answered my question, checked with Collis, and agreed to meet me at the Raskin house.

Arriving there, I found her parked down the road. Opening the door of her car, now all in working order and smelling faintly of the motor mechanic from the Calistoga garage, I climbed inside, kissed her, and grinned at the obvious curiosity which the half hour since we had spoken on the telephone had not cooled.

'You're sure?' I asked.

'Certain, and Jack Collis checked too. The Raskins had no children.'

I thought for a moment. 'Drive up to the house,' I said. 'I'll follow you. Two cars will make Karen think this is a big occasion.'

'Why do you want to . . . ' I closed the door, cutting off her question, patted the roof of the car, and went back to mine.

It was cruel, I suppose, putting heat on Karen Raskin in this way but there were too many oddities and until some of them were cleared out of the way nothing could be done about the really serious business of discovering who had tried to kill Victoria and succeeded in causing the death of Linda Lee Lewis.

By the time we had convoyed up to the house, slammed a few doors and eventually leaned heavily on the bell, Karen must have known trouble was on its way.

'We want to talk about your family,' I said, when she had let us into the house and we were all crammed into the tiny kitchen at the back.

'My family? There's no one, not now, not since . . . ' One hand gestured to the patch of grass out back which stretched down to the corrugated iron covered shed near where her brother Jimmy had died.

'No,' I said. 'Not Jimmy, not Pete.' Suddenly I knew there was no need for the heavy pressure. I reached out, took her hand and gently made her sit down at the kitchen table. Sitting opposite her, with Victoria standing out of Karen's sight at the far side of the room, the threatening atmosphere we had deliberately created dissipated. 'Tell us about the children, the boy and the girl.'

She looked at me in silence.

'What were their names?' I asked

Tears filled her eyes and slowly rolled down her cheeks. I let a couple of minutes drag by. It was almost completely silent. Even Karen's crying was noiseless.

'Tell us,' I said again.

She wiped a hand across her face, smearing bright patches of moisture. The angriness which had been a seemingly permanent feature of her expression, had gone. 'They didn't have names,' she said. 'Not real names. They were never taken to church.'

'Go on, Karen.'

The two children had been born a year apart, no one had known Karen was pregnant and she had delivered both babies herself while her husband was working. The first child, a boy, had died within hours. In a state of mind she had difficulty describing even now, Karen had insisted on keeping the baby close to her. Peter had buried the tiny body beneath the floor of the shed.

The second birth, apart from the baby

being a girl, was almost a re-run of the first.

'Is that why Peter started shooting the night the police came?' I asked.

Karen nodded without speaking. I looked up at Victoria who turned her head away from me. No one was coming out of this with much joy.

'How about your brother Jimmy. Did he know about the babies?'

'Yes.' The word was little more than an exhalation of breath.

'And that's why he protected you, after Peter died.'

'He didn't know at first. I told him about five years ago. Gil wanted me to go away with him but I couldn't leave this house. Jimmy wanted me to go with Gil. I had to tell him, to explain why I couldn't leave.'

'Does Gil know?'

She shook her head and the tears rolled again.

Victoria came over to the table and put an arm around Karen's shoulders. She gave me a tiny nod of the head and I left them and went in search of the telephone.

I called Deputy Collis and told him to send a team out with shovels and the county coroner. He didn't ask any questions; the fact that Victoria had enquired earlier if the Raskins had any children would have set him thinking.

It was a couple of hours later before Victoria and I made it back to the Deputy's office. She had taken over Collis's room and every flat surface was covered in files and loose papers. One young Deputy, looking barely old enough to shave, was alone in the building while everyone else was out coping with the miniature crime wave which seemed to be growing behind our movements.

The absence of people meant that we could talk freely. Not that there was much to freely talk about. Victoria was having a hard time coming to terms with the fact that she might have put five bullets into a man whose main offence was protecting his wife.

'He did kill Gerry Mandan,' she said. It wasn't in reply to anything I had said, just a response to her own unspoken thoughts.

I didn't answer right away because I

had some other thoughts that I needed to pursue before putting into words. Instead, I told Victoria about Ruth Beckerman and Jane Cole.

'It's not against the law,' she said.

'I never said it was, I'm telling you so you can back out of that dinner invitation if you want to.'

'Why should I?' Something approaching a smile touched the corner of her mouth. 'Afraid I might succumb?'

'In a life where certainties vanish faster than smoke in a hurricane, that is one thing over which I will not lose any sleep. And speaking of losing sleep, I missed you last night.'

'Me too.'

I waved a hand at the files. 'What is there here?'

'Statements, medical examiners' reports on all the killings, fingerprints, every damn thing you can think of and none of it points a finger at anyone else.' She hesitated, then put a forced smile on her face. 'Truthfully, it doesn't point much of a finger at Peter Raskin either. What seemed like a big fat case ten years ago doesn't look so hot today.'

One bundle of files was bound in twine and had yet to be opened. 'What are they?' I asked.

'They arrived from LA just before you called me about Karen.'

I opened up the bundle and leafed through various papers.

'Are you looking for something special?' Victoria asked.

'Your partner's notebooks.'

She didn't ask why but took over the search and I left her to it. She knew what she was looking for, I didn't.

Instead, I turned to the local Sheriff's office reports and eventually found a thin file labelled 'Ballistics Report'; I would have felt happier if it had been thicker.

I read through the file and by the time I was finished, which didn't take very long, Victoria had come upon Gerry Mardan's diary.

I read the last couple of weeks, after first asking Victoria at what point they had begun to home in onto Peter Raskin.

Then I made coffee for us both, firmly closed the door to ensure the morose young Deputy couldn't hear, and set out a few half-baked theories.

Gerry Mandan had indicated that he wanted more information from Ruth Beckerman, the psychiatrist, who had talked with Peter Raskin. But the young policeman had not had time to talk with her again, so we had no means of knowing what his ideas had been. I could ask Ruth Beckerman if she had any clues, but it didn't seem very likely. For all I knew, Gerry's idea might well have been a flight of fancy with no foundation in reality. And, of course, it was now also ten years old.

The ballistics reports were sparse. A bullet had been dug out of Gerry Mandan but it was badly damaged and the report had contented itself with confirmation of calibre. Another bullet, taken from the fleshy part of the wounded patrolman's shoulder had been checked as having come from Peter Raskin's gun.

'I think we need to do two things,' I said to Victoria. 'You backtrack through Mandan's diary and, where you can, talk with the people he talked to ten years ago. It's pretty hopeless, I know, but go through the motions as if it had all happened yesterday. See if you can build up what was in his mind those last couple of weeks. That way, you might be able to figure what questions he wanted to ask Ruth Beckerman. Then, when we go to dinner we'll have something to talk about apart from her sex life.'

'Okay, I'll try but it won't be easy. What's the other thing?'

'I want to talk with Collis and find out what happened to these two bullets.'

'Why?'

'I think we need a more detailed report than we have here.'

'The bullets are at the coroner's office in St Helena. Collis volunteered that but I didn't think we would need them.'

'Can you have them sent over?'

'Any tests will have to be done there, there are no facilities here in Calistoga.'

'I think I'll feel happier with them here. When we need to, we can take them back for testing in our presence.'

'You're not turning paranoid, are you?'

'Even paranoids need to take precautions.'

'Okay, if it keeps you happy.'

After she had made the call we went outside and had just decided to take my car, or to be precise about ownership, Sam Monahan's car, when a horn tooted the first few bars of a rude song at us. The car responsible, a shining red Firebird, pulled over and Holly Monahan leaned out. Today she was wearing a chunky sweater that looked much too warm for the weather. It was in her favourite red and matched the car. Sitting beside her was Cliff Monahan, also dressed casually. His biscuit-coloured sweater looked like cashmere and had probably cost as much as my air fare over here.

'We're partying tonight,' Holly called. 'You're invited and there is no such word as no.' She smiled at me in a way calculated to melt the fillings in my teeth.

I could hear Victoria's breathing quicken and rested a hand on her arm before she took a poke at the young actress. 'What's the occasion?' I asked.

'I've been told I'm in *Harper's Valley*

for the rest of the current series, my part
is being built up, and I've signed to do a
movie in Colorado during the winter
when we break for six weeks from the
show. I am rich, and the whole goddamn
world is beating a path to my door'

I looked at her husband to see how he
was taking the good news. His smile was
cheerfully genuine. He seemed to approve
of the fact that his wife was about to be
famous, independently wealthy, and the
object of sexual fantasising by any male
who owned a TV set.

'The party's at the Country Club,'
Holly chattered on. 'Ten o'clock. Okay?'

Before I had time to answer Cliff cut
in. 'There's Ruth now.'

Down the street, Ruth Beckerman and
Jane Cole were climbing out of an
oversize station wagon.

'We must go,' Holly said. 'We have to
invite them too. Everyone will be there.'

Across the street from Ruth Beckerman's office a man was stepping out of a
car. He walked over towards the two
women and although we were much too
far away to see facial expressions, let

alone hear words, it was clear that the man and the psychiatrist knew one another.

'We'll be happy to come to your party,' I told Holly. She and Cliff waved their appreciation of my courtesy and headed their car for the little group beside the station wagon.

'For God's sake . . . ' Victoria began but I cut her off and pulled her quickly into my car. From there I pointed at the yellow-haired man who was now recrossing the street to his car while the Monahans talked with Ruth Beckerman and Jane Cole.

Victoria looked at Markowitz, then at Ruth Beckerman, then at me. 'What the hell is going on here?' she asked.

I started the car and headed down Lincoln in the direction of St Helena. 'It beats me,' I admitted. 'But one thing's for sure, as parties go, tonight's should prove more interesting than most.'

19

The Lakeside Country Club was not what I expected. Back home, country clubs tend to be restored early-Victorian houses, probably originally built by textile barons and the like. They have gone through a variety of lives including army headquarters, private schools, pop stars' residences, and squatters' pads before being taken up by some entrepreneur with delusions of becoming famous for his, or his chef's flambéed strawberries.

The lake in question was Lake Berryessa and the club was a modern building designed in such a spectacular manner that Spock would feel at home in it. The one with the pointed ears, not the one who knew about babies.

It looked as though Holly Monahan had invited everyone she had passed in the street. No one stood guard at the door to weed out undesirables, gatecrashers and those who had anticipated the evening's revelries by getting steamed before arrival.

A band was playing on the lawn; all electronics, flashing lights and multi-decibel clamour. I don't know what the tune was and I doubt if the musicians did either. They looked as if they too had been at the hard stuff: and not just booze.

What the club members thought about it all, heaven alone knows. Presumably Monahan money had crossed a few palms and they had all stayed home.

Holly and Cliff Monahan were carrying out the duties of host and hostess but something, maybe only adrenalin, was flowing through Holly's veins and standing at the door kissing cheeks didn't seem to be holding much attraction for her.

'The hell with it,' she declared to no one in particular 'Let them all come.' She eyed me speculatively. 'I feel like dancing.'

Even if Victoria hadn't been there I wouldn't have volunteered. My decidedly limited capacity in that field of human endeavour wouldn't stand a prayer with the kind of music that was careening off into the night sky like a newly-launched space probe. 'Not me,' I told her, trying to sound filled with regret.

'There's Larry,' Cliff said, pointing out an athletic-looking blond youth whose legs were twitching to the music as he stood alone near the dance floor.

Holly didn't need second-telling and soon she and the blond youth were performing something that looked kin to an ancient fertility rite.

'Holly's terrific, isn't she,' Cliff said, the admiration in his voice undoubtedly sincere.

It seemed to me that in marrying a girl like Holly he had assured himself of endless problems in the future but I didn't say so. 'Come and have a drink,' I said instead.

A bartender made drinks for the three of us with Victoria settling for something non-alcoholic. I didn't want to be impaired either but I risked my alertness with a well-watered bourbon. Cliff took the same but stronger. Maybe he was being disloyal to the company's product but I had the feeling that Laronne's best was not on hand for tonight's party. He raised his glass towards Holly who was dancing by and she rewarded him with a twirl that displayed her slender tanned thighs. The young man she was dancing with was twitching more than his legs now.

I looked at Cliff who was smiling lovingly at his wife. Some people can't recognise trouble even when they sleep with it.

He saw me looking his way. 'How're you making out with the opposition?' he asked.

'Progressing,' I said cautiously. There was no reason not to tell him, but out of courtesy I wanted to talk to his father first. I was also more than a mite uneasy at some of the loose ends which still needed knotting.

'It must be interesting,' he remarked.

'What must?'

'Your work.'

'It doesn't make you rich,' Victoria said.

He shrugged. 'What's so good about being rich?'

We stared at him, then I caught a glimmer of amusement at the back of his eyes and we all laughed.

'Yes,' he said, 'I have to admit that being rich does have its advantages.' He glanced across to Holly again. 'It's better now I have Holly, but until she came along I think I would've preferred spending my life running the Half Note.'

That gave me an opening. 'How well did you know Peter Raskin?'

He looked at me curiously over the top of his glass. His eyes, light-brown and usually untroubled, clouded slightly. 'Not too well. Why do you ask?'

'I'm interested in him.'

'So I hear, but why ask me?'

'He played the piano in your club.'

He sipped at his drink. 'I didn't think you were interested in his musical ability.'

'I'm not.'

'Then I can't help you. He came to the club every night for a couple of years, played his set, and went home again. I don't even know where home was, except that it was somewhere in Alameda. The only time I ever saw him outside the club was one time when he came out to Laronne with a band. Sam was throwing a party . . . for Laraine. He asked me to provide the music. I know that was the night Peter met Karen. She worked for my father's company. Not long after that they were married.'

'And you lost a piano player.'

'It didn't make much difference. A month after that party Laraine was dead and I decided to fold the club and come back to Laronne. I thought my father could use a little help.'

'When was this?' Victoria asked.

'Twelve years ago.' He thought for a moment. 'Almost exactly.'

'Do you think Peter Raskin killed all those women?'

Cliff called over one of the overworked bartenders, who were not too busy to keep an eye on the man paying tonight's wages, and ordered a refill. 'I can't give you an informed opinion; like I said, I barely knew him, but he seemed too . . . gentle.' He shrugged. 'That sounds pretty stupid, I know. I guess half the mass-murderers in history were quiet on the outside, otherwise they wouldn't have got away with it long enough to become mass-murderers, would they?'

'No, I don't suppose they would,' Victoria said softly.

'Sorry I can't be more help.'

'That's okay.' I saw Ruth Beckerman coming into the bar looking faintly bemused at the overcrowded, overheated and much too noisy atmosphere Cliff Monahan saw me looking, glanced the same way and smiled and waved to the psychiatrist. She came over, seemingly relieved at the appearance of three normal people in a mass of what were rapidly becoming very drunk, loud-talking exhibitionists. There were enough couples doing everything but get laid, to suggest that before the night was over a porno movie-maker could clean up just by pointing a camera and letting nature take its course.

'I'm pleased you're here,' I told Ruth. 'I thought we might take up your invitation to dinner sometime soon. We could use some professional advice.'

'You're still looking into Peter Raskin's case?'

'Yes.'

'What do you think, Ruth?' Cliff asked her. 'Do you think he could do things like that?'

Ruth Beckerman shrugged her shoulders, screwed up her face and thought hard. 'I already told Mr Mace that I do not know what would make a man kill all those women, but, if you want a very unprofessional response it would have to be that Peter did not have any of the outward appearances of a mass-killer.' She smiled. 'But then, if he had the outward appearance of one he wouldn't have lasted long enough to *become* one, would he?'

Cliff Monahan nodded agreement at this almost word-for-word agreement with his opinion.

'But we can still meet and talk?' I asked.

'Of course. How would tomorrow evening suit?'

A glance at Victoria told me she was happy with that. We settled on a time. I already had the address from Ruth's business card but she insisted on giving me detailed directions which sounded pretty complicated.

'Oh shit,' Cliff Monahan said.

I looked at him, then followed the direction of his irritated look. Charles Gatliff, Holly's co-star on *Harper's Valley* was weaving a highly erratic course towards the bar.

'I think I might need a helping hand to keep him from wrecking the place.' Cliff said to Ruth. 'Enjoy yourselves,' he added to us before leading her through the crush to where Gatliff was mauling a young woman who seemed not to mind in the least but whose escort was clearly considering which part of the actor's anatomy to hit first.

'I think I've had enough of this,' Victoria said.

I had too but I looked around in case anything or anyone popped out of the woodwork to make the evening something less than a complete waste of time.

I was surprised to see Deputy Collis, looking no less a law enforcement officer out of uniform than he did when on duty. 'Jesus,' he said, as he joined us. 'If I'd known it was this kind of shindig I would've stayed home and watched TV.'

'Holly got to you, did she?' Victoria asked.

'She has an effect on a man,' Collis said.

'So I've noticed,' she said with a sidelong glance at me.

I grinned at her, refusing to be drawn.

'Is your wife here?' Victoria asked.

'She had a headache.' Collis laughed. 'Smart move'. He suddenly changed his expression. 'We dug up the floor of the Raskin garage,' he said. 'Two bodies, skeletons really. Tiny. I don't know, maybe a few weeks old.'

'What did Karen say?'

'It looks as if she might have done it, suffocated them. That, or maybe crib death. At this stage we'll have to go on what her lawyer tells her to say in court. I think, if we'd leaned on her, we could have got a confession.' He shrugged, looking at the milling, noisy, excitedly drinking throng. 'What the hell, it was a long time ago.' He gestured at the people around us. 'I guess they've all got a few bodies of one kind or another buried someplace. For me, Karen Raskin's already had it bad enough without going to trial on this.' He looked at Victoria with sudden concern. 'I didn't mean anything by that.'

'I know you didn't, Jack.'

'By the way, that guy you asked us to watch at the Mount View Hotel isn't using the name Markowitz but we're watching the right guy, your description was good. Anyway, as I was coming over here I talked over the horn to my man. Markowitz is at Ruth Beckerman's house. That assistant of hers, Jane Cole, let him in. Seemed to know him.' He looked around and located Ruth who, with Cliff, was guiding a shaky-legged Charles Gatliff out towards some fresh air. He didn't appear too enthusiastic at the prospect of filling his lungs with something to which he was possibly allergic. 'Do you think we should tell Dr Beckerman? If this guy is up to something maybe that assistant is in trouble, or tied in with him which could be just as bad.'

'No,' I said. 'I think it would be a very

bad move to tell Dr Beckerman anything at the moment.'

Collis looked at me speculatively for a moment, then nodded slowly. He glanced around the room. 'I think I'll have a beer then go home. This isn't the kind of place I want to be when the roof falls in.'

I knew what he meant. Social life for a cop can be a highly delicate area. Busting people you drink with is bad for the image.

'I think we should leave,' I said to Victoria as Collis pushed his way towards the bar.

'I'm glad to hear you say it, the hotel is suddenly very inviting.'

'Not there, not right away.'

'Now what are you scheming?'

'I'll tell you when we're out of this mob.'

Outside, Charles Gatliff had survived the fresh air, and was performing a sort of dance with Holly and the blond young man with whom she had been cavorting. The young man wasn't looking too pleased about it but Holly had a tolerant smile on her face. Cliff Monahan and

Ruth Beckerman were on hand in case the actor fell over or threw up but for the moment at least he appeared in control of his vital functions and was enjoying the stir he was creating among the other guests.

The parking lot was some distance away and no one noticed us drive off.

The instructions Ruth Beckerman had given me were complicated because so too was the way to her house. It was tucked away in a tiny clump of pines down at the bottom of a narrow lane. Other houses studded the sides of the lane and most of them too were surrounded by trees.

'Why?' Victoria asked as we parked the car in someone's driveway entrance and walked carefully along in the dark.

'Curiosity,' I said.

'You know what that did.'

'I know.'

'I can't believe that Ruth Beckerman's involved in an attempt to extort money from Sam Monahan?'

'I have to admit it doesn't seem very likely but why else would she associate with Markowitz?'

'Search me.'

I reached out and found her hand. 'Later,' I said.

A large figure loomed out of the darkness. It was the gloomy young Deputy I'd seen at Collis's office. It seemed he always drew the ratty jobs. Most police departments have a young officer on the strength for precisely such purposes.

I told him we'd just talked with Collis and were taking over. He wasn't too sure but he clearly had better ways of spending what was left of the night and silently and quickly he talked himself into leaving.

20

Ruth Beckerman's house was small, neat and expensive-looking with a mass of flowering plants either growing around or rambling over it. In sunlight it must have looked perfect for the cover of one of those magazines which exist to show people how lousy their own drab lives are by depicting the lifestyles of other, richer people. In the cool darkness the flowers gave off a thick, heady perfume that was more suited to an evening of romance Hollywood-style than to creeping around the way we were.

Curtains were pulled across all the windows at ground level and only from one did a tiny glow of light show through. The front door was locked, so too were the doors into the kitchen and from the empty garage into the house. Markowitz's car was parked hard up to one wall and when I spotted a partly open window on the upper floor I used the car as a stepping-stone. Moments later I was inside and helping Victoria scramble through.

'I'd feel better about this if I knew why we're breaking the law,' she whispered.

'Ringing the doorbell doesn't seem the way to go about it,' I said softly.

'Go about what?'

'Discovering just how friendly Markowitz is with Ruth Beckerman and Jane Cole.'

I led the way on a quick survey of the upper rooms, all of which were empty, then down the stairs. The room from which light had gleamed through the heavy drapes was at the back of the house. Through the door I could hear music, soft and tinkly. The adjoining room was the kitchen and we went in there. A hatch with sliding doors was cut through the dividing wall. Very cautiously I eased them open. The carpenter who had made them must have been good at his job because they moved silently. An inch or so was enough to let us see through.

The music was coming from a TV set

which was mounted above a video recorder. A video film was playing. It was decidedly pornographic. Three men were subjecting a young woman to several things which would have been extraordinary one at a time. Simultaneously, they made her into some kind of superstar.

What was happening on the floor in front of the TV set was also extraordinary and if it wasn't pornographic that's only because I don't think the word applies to such activities in the flesh. And in the flesh they were. I had my answer as to how friendly Markowitz was with Jane Cole. Very friendly. Well, of all forms of intercourse, the anal variety needs either close cooperation or has to be achieved at gun or knife point. Markowitz wasn't using a gun or a knife and Jane Cole was giving all the signs and sounds of enjoying every inch of his efforts.

I stood back from the slit in the hatch and looked at Victoria. The gleam of light which came through into the kitchen wasn't enough to read her expression and we couldn't talk about it. I risked closing the hatch, then drew her to the far side of the room. 'I don't think they'll be talking too much,' I whispered.

She shook her head.

'So, unless you think we can learn anything else . . . '

'The hell we can,' she hissed back.

We had moved to the door which led from the kitchen to the garden when we heard the sound of a car approaching. Cautiously, I felt for a key, turned it and eased the door open. Then we waited. It was clear that the car was being driven into the garage. It appeared that Ruth Beckerman was home.

I slipped back to the hatch and opened it again. Jane Cole and Markowitz were still coupled together. If Ruth came into the kitchen we would have to leave fast by the back door and hope she didn't catch us. If she went into the other room we would have a grandstand seat at what might well turn out to be an informative encounter.

She didn't come into the kitchen; she went into the other room. We did have a grandstand seat and it was an encounter that told us quite a lot; but it was not what either of us expected.

The door into the other room was not visible from the gap in the serving hatch. As a result. Ruth was well inside before she came into view.

She stood for a moment, watching the naked bodies on the floor in front of the TV set, then sat on the arm of a light yellow leather couch. Her expression was . . . interested.

Then Jane Cole opened her eyes and saw her employer. She smiled and reached out a hand. Ruth touched the outstretched hand briefly, then stood up and hurriedly undressed. Moments later she carefully knelt astride Jane's head and lowered herself down.

After a while, when Markowitz was forced to withdraw to the sidelines to restore himself, Ruth and Jane continued. Quite clearly this was no new experience for the two women.

Markowitz was drinking heavily and a little later Jane rummaged through her discarded clothes for a joint. All three of them smoked, handing the joint back and forth. Markowitz proved he was not a regular at these sessions by suggesting that he and Ruth should screw. Her response was curtly negative. Obviously Ruth was not into men; put another way, she didn't want men into her.

It was maybe another hour during which more grass was smoked and more booze sunk and more variations tried out and more video films screened before the three performers passed out from too much of one thing or another.

'I think we should take a look around,' I said. My voice sounded thick in my ears.

Victoria didn't speak at all.

I risked putting on lights as we checked through the upstairs rooms once more. One room was arranged as a study with a couple of small filing cabinets. One was locked and I used my already damaged penknife to prise open the bottom drawer.

The drawer was filled with files, each one labelled with a person's name. I glanced in one or two and it became quickly apparent that these were patients of Ruth Beckerman's but from handwritten notes on the inside cover they were either very rich or had other advantages which the psychiatrist thought important enough to warrant special treatment and filing away from the office and potential prying eyes.

This drawer held the alphabet from N to Z and I looked for Peter Raskin but he wasn't there. I opened the drawer above, making more noise than I had the first time. Victoria went to the head of the stairs, listened, then came back. 'All quiet,' she said softly.

The only name on the files in this drawer which rang any bells was the last one. I took it out and opened it, wondering why Laraine Monahan qualified for special treatment and, for that matter, why she had been a patient of the psychiatrist.

From the basic facts at the head of the file notes, the patient's date of birth among them, it was clear that this was the second Laraine, Cliff's step-mother, who had died in an airplane crash twelve years ago.

The case notes didn't amount to very much. Just comments upon the patient's behaviour and response to various tests which were meaningless to me and to Victoria.

'What do you think you're doing?' a voice said behind us.

Ruth Beckerman was at the door of the study. She had put her dress on again but that was not all; she'd taken time to pick up a weapon. It was a small calibre revolver, probably a .22, chromium-plated and pearl-handled. It would have been pretty if it hadn't been pointed at Victoria.

Ruth took in the damaged filing cabinet, then the file I was holding. She held out a hand for it. I didn't argue. At this range she could make a nasty hole in Victoria, even with a small bullet.

'So. You know about Laraine.'

I didn't know anything about Laraine but I didn't say so. Ruth was looking hazy, maybe she would talk. She did.

'She came to me because she needed help and I gave it to her. More than that, I gave her love.'

I thought about the scene below a little while earlier. 'You had an affair with her?' I asked.

'Affair? I loved her. But she wouldn't come to me. She said it was . . . unnatural.' She shook her head slowly from side to side as if trying to clear away the mists caused by the grass she had smoked. 'Then she died. Killed herself in her airplane. I went to Sam, offered him myself. I could have made him happy. He didn't need a young woman like Laraine. We could have been good together. But all he wanted was sex.' She made the word sound dirty. 'He asked me to be hostess at his business meetings, his parties, his dinners. Me, a hostess. I should have been part of it all. I should have had a share of Laronne for what I did for the Monahans, what I've continued to do for them.'

Ruth had moved further into the room and the gun was no longer pointing at Victoria who very cautiously stepped back a half pace.

'So you decided to take a share by other means.' I said.

She nodded. The gun was hanging straight down by her side now.

'Markowitz can't help you any more,' I said. 'He's on his own. His friends are under arrest.'

'I don't need them, I can do it alone.'

Victoria swung a sudden blow at Ruth, the edge of her hand chopping against her neck. The older woman stumbled sideways, the gun fell to the floor, and a row of books on a low table went flying.

I swept up the gun, dropped it into my pocket and headed for the stairs. I had guessed right, Markowitz had heard the noise and despite his condition was already into his pants when I went in through the door of the room.

I was across the floor as he reached for his coat, lying crumpled in a heap beside the TV set which was still showing images of complex intertwinings of human bodies. I hit him hard, hurting my knuckles on the side of his face. He went down and I picked up the coat, feeling the heavy weight of something I guessed was a gun. This one was much bulkier and more lethal than Ruth Beckerman's toy.

'What's happening, wha . . . ' Jane Cole was staring up at me from where she had passed out on the floor. Somehow she seemed to recognise me, or maybe she just recognised a man and in her state of mind any one was as good, or as bad, as any other. 'Hi,' she said and smiled dreamily, spreading her legs in what might have been an inviting fashion if I hadn't seen the amount of activity that part of her had been subjected to tonight.

I was careless, looking at her when Markowitz was still conscious. I sensed rather than saw or heard him coming at me and swung round in time to duck a punch he threw at my head. There was an angry red mark on his cheek, contrasting vividly with his pale complexion. I took the gun from the pocket of his coat and hit him with it, very hard, just behind the ear. He went down with a crash, falling over the video recorder. He must have hit the pause button because the image on the screen froze on a young woman's pose of simulated ecstasy.

Jane screamed, once and not especially loudly. I reached down and turned off the recorder and the TV.

'You mix with bad company,' I said. I found her clothes, a suit similar to the one I'd seen her wear before. I tossed them to her. 'Time to get dressed, the party's over.'

'What's all the noise about down here?' Victoria asked from the door.

'This end is tied up, how's Ruth?'

'I think I must have hit her harder than I intended. Either that or the smoking and drinking has finally got to her.'

'What do you want?' A tiny voice asked. Jane was partially dressed now and looking rather ill.

'Do you know what you're mixed up in?'

She shook her head.

'Extortion, hijacking, various kinds of violence to property and to people. Maybe more when we open it all up.'

'I didn't know. I didn't. I came as Ruth's assistant. We . . . well, she said she liked me . . . you know. We became lovers. I liked her, admired her. She didn't mind if I went with men.'

'Big-hearted of her,' I said.

I found a necktie among Markowitz's clothes and bound his hands behind his back.

'What happens to him?' Jane asked.

'Tonight, prison. Later, with luck, a lot more of the same.'

'What will happen to me?'

Before I had time to speculate for her a car engine fired into life outside. Victoria turned and was halfway up the stairs by the time I reached the front door. I pulled it open in time to see Ruth Beckerman's car career out of the garage, swing around in a half circle, and then rocket away through the gate and down the narrow road.

21

I went back inside to meet Victoria as she came down the stairs.

'Sorry,' she said. 'I really thought she was out.'

'No matter.' In the main room I checked Markowitz was safe, then brought Jane Cole into the hallway and pushed her ahead of me up the stairs.

In the study I picked up the fallen books and let the young woman sit in the only chair. She was pale and close to tears. What was happening around her had begun to penetrate. She looked very young and defenceless but I wasn't feeling open-hearted.

Victoria had followed us up the stairs. 'I'll call Collis,' she said. 'He can put out an apb.'

'He's probably home now. Let him rest. We can take Markowitz in and I want to talk to Sam Monahan before he hears it from Collis.'

I checked the filing cabinet drawers again, then picked up Laraine Monahan's file from the floor.

'What do you know about these files?' I asked Jane.

'I haven't seen them before,' she told me and it didn't sound like a lie. It made sense; Ruth wouldn't want anyone to know what she had in here, especially if she was using the files for illegal purposes.

I did my stuff with the penknife on the top drawer. There were more files and some old leather-bound desk diaries. One of the files was labelled with Peter Raskin's name. I leafed through the diaries but a quick glance showed nothing other than appointments.

Victoria checked Raskin's file. 'I never saw this before,' she said. 'Gerry alone saw Dr Beckerman at her office. She must have shown him this file and he made his notes from it.'

'We'll take everything with us.'

She nodded and we began lifting files out. After a moment or two she stopped to flick through a couple of them, then turned back again to Peter Raskin's. I could see a tiny crease cutting the skin between her eyebrows.

'Problem?' I asked.

'I'm not sure,' she said, glancing at Jane Cole.

I didn't press her. She would have a reason for not talking in front of the girl.

We ferried files, the girl, then Markowitz, out to the front lawn and I stood guard while Victoria brought the car up the lane.

Half an hour later we were in Collis's office with the bemused young Deputy locking Markowitz in one cell and Jane Cole in another.

Victoria riffled through the files we had left spread about the office and began checking against the material we had brought from Ruth Beckerman's study.

When we were finished we had two things and neither one was very clear. Gerry Mandan's report following his examination of Ruth's case notes on Raskin were inaccurate.

'Gerry was always careful,' Victoria said. 'That's why I wasn't happy when I saw this.'

She showed me the file we had brought from the psychiatrist's study. Ruth had known about the dead babies, but there was more. The evidence of Peter Raskin's mental instability was quite clear in the file, less so in the dead police officer's report. Much less so.

'This could have happened if the file was extended after Gerry saw it,' Victoria said.

'But there was enough to send you after Raskin.'

'Implications. Strong ones, maybe, and all of which Gerry wrote down but with the qualification that they were speculative. According to this file it's a whole lot more than that. It's solid proof.'

'So you think she deliberately put you onto Raskin?'

She nodded. 'Then, when Peter and Gerry were both dead the case notes were extended to make it clear that he was the killer of all those women. She did that for when we went back to check.' She paused, her face set. 'But we didn't go back and check. I didn't.'

I waited

'So I killed an innocent man.'

'He shot Gerry.'

'To protect his wife whom he thought was responsible for the deaths of two babies.' She was taking it hard and I didn't add an earlier thought which I still had to check out. If what I was thinking proved right there was worse to come.

Picking up the ballistics reports I took another look at them, then I went out and asked the young Deputy if a package had come from the coroner's office. It had. The two bullets were both .38 calibre; one slightly twisted, the other just a shapeless piece of lead. It was easy to see why the ballistics examiner hadn't troubled to tackle the tricky problem of checking that both came from the same gun.

'Where are the coroner's reports?' I asked.

Victoria produced a thick pile. The top dozen were the dead women; down at the bottom were those on Peter Raskin, Gerry Mandan and the injured cop. I read these three carefully. I don't know much about medical matters but where they impinge on my world, which is all too often, I've learned to understand the long words.

'What are you looking for?' Victoria asked as I read the report on Raskin. I finished it without answering, then set it aside. I had been hoping for something that might give her a loophole through which to squeeze her conscience.

'He died because I shot him five times,' she said. 'There was nothing else.'

I should have known that she would've studied this one herself. 'Sorry,' I said.

I read through the others.

'Well?' Victoria asked when I was finished.

'I'm puzzled,' I said.

'Why?'

I laid the two bullets on the desk and pointed at the bent one. 'This hit the cop in the shoulder, damaged the bone although it didn't strike head on, and lodged in soft muscle.' I touched the distorted, splayed piece of lead few people would have recognised as a bullet. 'This one hit Gerry Mandan in the throat.' Victoria's eyes flickered as she

287

looked at it. I could tell that she was seeing her partner again. From the medical report it must have been a bloody mess. 'The bullet didn't hit the spinal column, yet it opened up like this. Almost as if it had been notched.'

She frowned. 'A dum-dum?'

I nodded.

'Why would Raskin . . . ' She stopped and picked up the bullet. All squeamishness vanished as professionalism took over. 'He wouldn't do that, and the chances of him acquiring a dum-dum bullet accidentally are slim.' She laid the bullet back on the table and eyed me speculatively 'You think there were two gunmen that night, right?'

'Yes, just as another man was there the night Jimmy Paine was shot.'

'Who?'

'God knows, but I'm sure there's a connection. The man who shot Gerry Mandan, the man shooting at us at Karen Raskin's house, the man who's been trying to kill you since you reached town are all connected. For all I know they could all be the same man.'

'Why?'

'Well, if someone other than Peter Raskin shot Gerry Mandan ten years ago that person would be decidedly jumpy when you came back to Calistoga. Maybe he thought that he hadn't got away with it after all, that despite all the years of living free the law was about to catch up with him.'

'And not just for the killing of Gerry Mandan. He had to have a reason for that.'

I nodded agreement.

'Whoever it was also killed all those women,' Victoria said quietly.

'Could be,' I said.

'But I was working on the same case. Why didn't he try to kill me then, instead of waiting ten years?'

'Because it was Gerry who was the threat, not you. Gerry knew something you didn't.'

Victoria shook her head. 'I don't think so. We shared ideas, information, there was no competition between us. Gerry wasn't like that and neither was I.'

'Maybe,' I said.

'I'm sure of it.'

There was a rattle at the door and the young Deputy came in looking flushed. 'That girl's giving trouble back there,' he told us. 'She won't stop crying.'

We went through to the cells. There were four of them, all heavily barred but allowing all occupants to see one another. Markowitz was lying on the pull-down bed in one, hands clasped behind his head and staring at Jane Cole who was crunched up into a tiny ball in the furthermost corner of her cell.

Markowitz glanced our way as we came through the heavy metal door and grinned lazily.

'Take her into the office,' I told the young Deputy. 'You talk to her, calm her down,' I added to Victoria. 'I'll have a word with our friend here.'

I waited until the yellow-haired man and I were alone. The cells were very clean and had an unlived-in air about them. I guess that Calistoga didn't have a very high crime rate.

'What did you say to her?' I asked.

'Me?' He had a contented smile on his face.

'Don't play smart, Markowitz. You're in very bad trouble.'

'Not me. Anyway, all I did was tell her how she could make money in the movie business. That's where I plan to take her when we get out of here. I have a couple of guys who will fix her so she'll never want to see an old dyke like Ruth Beckerman ever again. You know what I mean? Big guys, guys who'll impress her very deeply.' He laughed and there was no humour in it.

'What makes you think you'll be getting out?' I asked.

'What have I done?'

'You've been playing at hijacker, extortioner, maybe a couple of other things as well.'

'Prove it.'

'Your friends have been picked up.'

He didn't like that but he was still unworried. 'So what? Koven has a small mind. I did all the . . . ' He broke off and laughed again. 'Hey, now, I nearly said something I shouldn't.'

'Go ahead, laugh, make your plans. You're not getting out for a long, long time. You made a bad mistake, all of you.'

His grin faded, then came back again. 'Don't try putting one over, Mace. I'll be out of here by morning.'

'No you won't. Not tomorrow morning, not any morning. You're involved in a murder case, Markowitz.'

'Murder? Nobody's been killed.'

'Wrong. At the last count seventeen people have died and all but one was murdered.'

'Don't try ... ' Markowitz's voice trailed off. He could see that I wasn't making jokes. 'I don't know what the hell you're talking about.'

'I believe you, but it doesn't matter a damn if I do or don't.'

'What do you want?'

'If you get out of here, you leave Jane Cole alone.'

'Sure, no problem. There are others.' He made it sound as though he could pick up any number of girls for his porno movie interests, or for any other area of the flesh trade. I suppose he and his kind always could.

'Tell me about Ruth Beckerman,' I said.

'What's to tell. Someone on the make. She came onto Koven asking for help in some deal she had worked out. He needed extra hands and I provided them.'

'Do you know anything else about her?'

He shook his head. I wouldn't have trusted him any further than I could heave the Transamerica Pyramid but he had no need to lie about this. If he thought he could throw someone to the wolves he'd do it.

'Any idea where she would go?'

'No.'

'Okay,' I said. 'If you want advice, don't be in too big a hurry to call a lawyer. As long as you're in here you can't be held responsible for anything else that happens.'

I left him to think about that. Either way, he wasn't a problem but if he was safe in a cell at least I could talk to him again if it became necessary.

Jane Cole had calmed down a little. I told her that Markowitz wouldn't come near her after all this was over.

I thought about the first time I had seen her and Ruth Beckerman in the office overlooking Lincoln. I asked her where the two of them had been the evening Victoria arrived in Calistoga.

'At the office. We were working late on some case notes.'

'Did you see Lieutenant Bercovici?'

She frowned.

'This is the Lieutenant,' I told her.

She looked at Victoria and slowly nodded her head. 'Yes, we saw her.' Her skin darkened with embarrassment.

'Well?'

'Ruth was watching her as she came along the street. I was angry. She was so interested I thought that she knew you.' She looked up at Victoria, her flush deepening. 'I thought that you were one of her other . . . ' She broke off.

Well, now we knew who had seen and recognised Victoria that night and kicked this mess into life.

'Where do you think Ruth is now?' Victoria asked.

Jane's head shook from side to side. 'I'll

never see her again now, will I?'

It occurred to me that not only was she right but that would be the best thing that could happen to her but I didn't say so.

'Where might she be?' Victoria asked, reaching out to touch the younger woman gently on the shoulder.

I was suddenly aware of the scene that had played out before us as we had watched through the hatch at the psychiatrist's house. This girl was far from being the soft and tortured creature she was making herself out to be. The things she had let Markowitz and Ruth do to her, the things she had done to them, had shown her to be capable of putting her body to any use that suited her. I was about to drop the gentle approach when she responded to Victoria. 'I think she might have gone to Laronne.'

'Why?'

'She has a room there. She keeps clothes and all the things she would need if she was going away.'

It made sense and I should have thought about the Monahan house myself.

'Will that help you find her?'

'Maybe,' Victoria said.

'If it does, can I go free?'

Victoria looked at me. I shrugged. As far as I knew, Jane Cole hadn't done anything illegal and probably didn't know much about what was happening all around her. One thing her last question showed was that I'd been right in assessing her capacity for any manoeuvre that suited her own purpose. She was quite happy to dump Ruth if it ensured she was off the hook.

I turned to the young Deputy. 'Put her in the hotel,' I said. 'Markowitz's room is empty. But see she doesn't get any bright ideas, like leaving town. Okay?'

He didn't look too cheerful about taking more orders especially after we had displaced him from surveillance at a time when everything had hit the fan but he couldn't think of a polite way to object.

'Maybe you should call Collis,' I suggested. 'Tell him we're going to Laronne. It might be smart if he follows us out there.'

But not, this time, too fast on the trigger, I thought. But I didn't say so because it wasn't fair. Collis was unlikely to risk another Jimmy Paine-type killing.

22

We drove the ten miles to Sam Monahan's winery in silence. This time it was not one of those companionable silences we sometimes enjoyed. It was heavy, tense, and we both knew that any word might be the wrong one.

Swinging up the long tree-lined drive with the headlights counting off the white fenceposts I made a mental promise to Linda Lee Lewis. I don't suppose she would have thanked me for it; I doubted if she had been the vengeful type.

Lights were on all over the building, and men were loading trucks when we drove up.

Monahan was supervising the work himself and was surprised to see us.

'What's happening?' I asked.

'We're trying another way of getting loads past the hijackers. If we move everything out at night we can slip past them.'

'There's no need,' I told him. 'The hijackers have been arrested, you can forget them.'

He looked at me, then at Victoria. 'How come?'

'You asked me to take an interest. I have. They're off your back.'

'You dealt with the Organisation in one day?'

I smiled. 'I wish I could say I had but it wasn't the Organisation. It was a small-time operation. They conned you into thinking they were connected.'

'Are you sure?'

'Certain.'

'My God,' he said quietly.

'Is Ruth here?'

He nodded.

'It was all down to her, Sam,' I told him.

'Ruth?'

'I don't know the details, but she hired men to hijack your trucks and put the bite on you.' I described Koven, Markowitz, Carlos and Lew Santini, the dwarf. He'd never seen the little man but the others were his three visitors. I suppose they left

299

Santini behind because he didn't look much like everyone's image of a hit man.

'I don't believe it,' Sam said.

We both looked at him in silence.

'Oh, shit,' he said and turned to walk into the house. We followed.

'Where's her room?' Victoria asked.

'Second floor, she has a suite over the garage.'

We went up the stairs with Sam at the rear. I didn't want him getting in the way of any stray bullets if Ruth Beckerman began blasting away at us.

The suite was lavish and looked as if it had been hit by a hurricane. Someone had packed in a hurry but the bag was still there, in the middle of the floor, waiting to be strapped shut. We checked the three rooms that made up the suite but Ruth was missing.

'She heard us coming,' Victoria said as she came out of the bathroom.

I went back down the stairs moving fast and checked outside. I couldn't hear any sounds of car engines. I called out to Eddie, Monahan's principal heavy.

'Where's Dr Beckerman's car?' I asked him.

He pointed to a Camora down by the loading bays.

'Immobilise it,' I said. 'And see nobody takes any other vehicle.'

He looked at Sam who had followed me outside. Monahan must have given him a sign because Eddie didn't argue.

'Where could she be?' I asked Sam.

'How in hell should I know?' he said. He was irritable and obviously still trying to come to terms with his part-time hostess's duplicity.

'Come on, Sam.'

'Look, just let her get the hell away from here.'

'No.'

'Why not, goddamn it?'

'Because there are other things we need to talk about. Some important questions need answering and they make your problems here seem like grape pips.'

He stared into my face, abruptly turned and walked stiffly over to a door set in the wall beside the main buildings 'There's a basement level,' he said. 'Cellars run all

301

the way under here.'

I suddenly remembered that gelignite was stored in the cellars and reminded Victoria. 'Maybe we should tell Collis to bring the big boys along.'

She shook her head. 'No, the longer she has down there the more time she has to set up something really unpleasant.'

'Okay,' I said, trying to sound cheerful about the prospect of going down below into heaven knew what.

Sam Monahan insisted on coming with us. It was probably as well that he did because there was a maze of passageways below ground with rooms leading off all of them. We made a systematic sweep through the building, working inwards and trying to ensure we gave Ruth Beckerman no chance to sneak behind us.

No one was in the room where the gelignite was stored and I breathed a small sigh of relief but I didn't have long to enjoy the feeling.

We were entering the adjoining room, a long, low-ceilinged expanse filled with wine barrels, when all the lights went out. In the darkness I grabbed for Victoria and pulled her down to the cold stone floor, holding her close to me.

Then the lights came on again and Ruth was closing the door behind us. She had a smile on her face but I was more interested in the gun in her hand and the fact that it wasn't pointing at any of us. Instead, it was aimed into the waxed cardboard box she had clamped under her other arm. Even if I hadn't been able to guess, the box was clearly labelled with its contents.

'None of you move,' Ruth said quietly. 'If you try anything at all, like shooting me or making any sudden moves, this gun will go off and so shall we all.'

She was right, we would. In this confined space, regardless of how many sticks of gelignite there were in the box, we wouldn't stand a chance.

Very carefully, I climbed to my feet, helping Victoria up as I did so.

'Leave your guns on the floor,' Ruth said.

We did as we were told. The alternative would be to ensure that the vintage maturing in the casks all around us would be especially full-bodied.

'Ruth,' Sam said.

'Shut up,' she said. 'This is all your fault, every last part of it is down to you.'

'I don't understand,' he said. He looked curiously deflated, his bulky chest no longer straining the material of his clothes.

'If you hadn't married Laraine, none of it would have happened.' She looked upwards at the vaulted ceiling. 'All because you had to marry a woman called Laraine just so she would match the name of your damned empire.'

Sam stepped forward. I don't think he was planning on attacking her. He simply wanted to know what she was talking about.

Ruth didn't waste time asking his intentions. She took the gun from among the gelignite, shot at him once and had the gun back in the box before he hit the ground.

23

The bullet had hit Sam Monahan high in the shoulder and he was unlikely to die, provided he had treatment quickly. That didn't seem very likely.

'Let me help him,' Victoria said.

After a moment Ruth Beckerman nodded her permission. Kneeling by Sam's side, Victoria managed to pull him into a position where she could try stopping the blood flowing.

'Thanks,' Sam said.

I thought about trying to grab Ruth's box of explosive but I didn't let the thought hold very long. It was too great a risk and there was little to be gained by it. Right now, softly-softly was the way to handle her. The manual says so The manual also says you should speak to people with death wishes, and make them talk.

'What did Laraine have to do with it?' I asked. I didn't want Sam to hear this but there was no choice. 'You said you loved her.'

'I did.' She moved towards Sam, for the first time letting me have a clear sight of the door. There was no way I could get past her and outside; even if there had been a way I couldn't have taken it. 'I warned her against marrying you,' she continued. 'I told her you didn't love her, you just wanted a young woman around the place to prove your goddamn virility. And because she was named Laraine, you could make believe your first wife was still alive.'

Sam was looking up at her, his expression curiously relaxed. 'I gave Laraine all she could want,' he said softly. 'And she repaid me by having an affair.'

'No, Sam, you guessed wrong. Lariane was faithful to you. Too much so; it cost her life.'

'You're wrong.' Sam's breathing was bad. 'She kept secrets from me.'

'Sure she did,' Ruth said. 'She thought it would hurt you too much if she told you the truth. She didn't want to come between you and Cliff.'

'You mean she was having an affair with my son?' Sam tried to sit up straighter but Victoria held him still.

'An affair? No, Sam, Cliff wouldn't leave her alone. Once, he raped her. That was what she was keeping from you, why she came to me for help, and why she flew her airplane into a mountainside.' Her voice had risen steadily and was now a shout. 'I loved her, I wanted her. I could have made her happy but she had to kill herself. Then, when I came to you and let you know I was available, what did you do? You said I could be your hostess. Hostess! God damn you, Sam Monahan.'

I had cautiously moved until my foot was on the butt of my gun and I gently moved it around until it was positioned where I could scoop it up fast; but Ruth still had the gelignite with her revolver jammed firmly into its midst.

'It's time I had my share of your money and your power,' Ruth was saying. 'All I've done for you and your family.' She had said something like this before, in the study of her home. 'But I'll have it yet, Sam. With you dead, I'll have it all. I still have control where it counts.'

Sam Monahan moved slightly and pain twisted his face in a sudden grimace. Ruth's attention was still on him and for the first time since she had shot Sam the muzzle of her gun lifted out of the box. I could have waited but the chances of her relaxing completely were slim. I stooped fast, sweeping up the gun. Ruth started to turn towards me. Instinct made her point her gun at me and that was the chance I needed. I had my gun now and swung it hard at the elbow which held the waxed box to her side. The crack as I hit the bone was sharp and she screamed. The box fell and I kicked at it, sending it skidding far along the floor beneath the racks of wine barrels.

Then Ruth was at the door, snatching it open. She stepped halfway through it, then turned and began firing. I dived for Victoria, covering her body with mine but none of the bullets came even close. Suddenly, I knew what Ruth was firing at.

I rolled over, hoping to snap off a shot at her but then the gelignite exploded with a dull, ear-bending roar and Ruth disappeared backwards, slamming the door shut behind her as she went.

There was smoke and debris flying through the air and hazing in the glow of the lamps slung low from the ceiling. Then there was another noise, a rushing, liquid sound.

The explosion had burst open barrels and vats of wine and it was pouring towards us in a frothing tide.

I grabbed at the door and turned the handle but it wouldn't open. Ruth had waited long enough to turn the key. Unless something happened, and happened fast, we stood a better than even chance of emulating the Duke of Clarence.

I helped Victoria lift Sam Monahan and carry him to a heavy wooden table stacked with what appeared to be testing equipment. I swept everything to the floor to make space for him, then turned to see what was happening along the cellar.

I couldn't see how many barrels and vats were damaged and it was impossible to guess whether there was enough wine flowing freely to really make drowning a possibility.

Then, above the liquid's rush I heard someone banging at the door. A woman's voice, high-pitched, shouting. 'It's locked,' I yelled.

'There's no key.' I recognised the voice. Holly Monahan was home from her party.

I looked at Sam. His eyes were closed and he was breathing hard, his face pale. He would be no help. 'Is there another way out?' I shouted.

'I don't know?'

'Another key?'

'I don't know.'

'Find Eddie,' I called.

But there was no need. Eddie had heard the explosion and accustomed to action even more than he was to taking orders, he had made his own moves. I saw him come into view like a pantomime devil in reverse as a hatch opened to admit a slowly descending barrel hoist.

We began carrying Sam across the floor and halfway there Eddie took over from Victoria. Moments later we were in the main courtyard of the vineyard, wet and cold and smelling of non-vintage grape juice.

'Did you do this?' Eddie asked.

He meant did we shoot Sam. 'No,' I told him, taking care to look him right in the eye.

'Then who did?'

'I don't think you'll believe this,' I said.

'Try me.'

'Ruth Beckerman.'

'You kidding me?'

'No.'

He looked at me for a moment, hard, then nodded. He made a couple of curt gestures. Men were there without words being spoken, and Sam Monahan was lifted into a car. Two of the men stayed with Sam and the car disappeared smoothly down the long curving driveway.

Moments later Holly came out of the building, her glittering party dress smeared with dirt. 'What happened?' she asked. 'Why did Ruth have a gun?'

'It's a long story. Where did Ruth go?'

'She went with Cliff in our car. We

arrived, heard an explosion and then she came out. He did just as she said. What's it all about?'

I ignored her question. 'Where did they go?'

She gestured towards a roadway which swung up the hillside behind the house.

'Let's go,' Victoria said.

The four of us crowded into the Chevy. I fired the motor and hit the accelerator. We squirted gravel as we headed upwards.

Early streaks of greenish-blue light were brightening the sky to the east. It looked like being another sunny Californian day.

'Are there any turnings off?' I asked Eddie.

'Not until we hit the highway.'

I went faster. So fast that I almost hit Ruth Beckerman.

She was on her hands and knees, crawling along the road ahead of us.

I slid the car to a standstill and we clustered around her.

She looked up at us, her face twisted with the effort of her attempt to escape, a myriad of tiny lines removing any last traces of good looks. There was blood on her clothes and for a moment I thought that she had been injured in the explosion.

Then, as Victoria reached down to her and pushed aside the collar of her stained dress I could see that she hadn't been hurt by her own attempts to kill us. Ruth Beckerman had been shot at close-range, and I didn't need a degree in medicine to know that she was dying.

24

'What happened? Who shot you?' Victoria asked.

Ruth didn't answer. Her face was distorted with pain.

Victoria looked at me. 'Cliff?' she asked.

It had a certain logic to it.

'What do you mean?' Holly asked.

I took hold of Ruth by the shoulders and pulled her face close to mine. 'You're dying,' I told her. 'What happened?'

Behind me I heard Victoria telling Eddie to bring medical help but she was just going through the motions and we all knew it. After a moment Ruth smiled and she knew it too.

'After Cliff raped Laraine he came to me.' She laughed. It was a rough, papery sound. 'I hated him for that. When Laraine died he blamed himself and I made sure he suffered. It was through him that I lost her.'

Blood bubbled at the corner of her mouth. A hand reached past me and gently wiped the blood away with a handkerchief. I glanced at Holly who was doing this and tried to read her expression. There was a maturity there that hadn't been present before Next time she had a serious role to play she might be able to bring to it something that her *Harper's Valley* stint didn't call for.

Ruth began speaking again, her voice fainter now but the grimace of pain had smoothed. Shock had proved its value as a painkiller. 'After Laraine died Cliff was broken with grief for more than two years. That was why he began killing those women.'

'Why for God's sake?'

'They'd all lost relatives, loved ones. He wanted to spare them the pain he'd felt.' She coughed and blood showed. 'He believed he'd committed incest, that Laraine was his mother. I made sure he kept on believing that.'

I was pleased now that she was dying. People had gone to her for help and as a result of her abuse of their trust many had died. Her profession had its share of charlatans, the way every profession does. It would survive but someone like Ruth Beckerman would take a deal of living down.

There was still one thing I didn't understand. 'Why did he shoot you? What's changed, why have you lost control of him?'

Her eyes were glazing now but she made an effort at focussing on Holly. 'There's only you in my way. I told him you had to die but he wouldn't do it.'

I heard a car coming up the road from the house. Eddie was back. I straightened up and as I did so Ruth Beckerman's fingers tightened on mine. I looked down at her.

'I loved her,' she said. 'I wanted her. I could have made her so happy.'

Then her fingers relaxed their grip and her hand fell away. Her eyes closed and her head rolled sideways. Ruth Beckerman had extended the death list she had helped create.

I brushed gravel from my clothes,

looked at Holly, then at Victoria. 'Let's go find him.' I said.

'Another car's coming up from the house,' Eddie said. 'You take this one. Do you need any help?'

'I'll call you if I do. You take care of Sam. Don't tell him any of this until he's well.'

'You don't have to tell me that,' he said, sounding mildly affronted.

I opened the car door for Holly.

'Is this wise?' Victoria asked.

'I think she might help,' I said. 'If Cliff thinks so much about her that he killed Ruth then we might be able to prevent any more deaths.'

I don't think I sounded very convincing. I certainly didn't convince myself, but Victoria nodded and didn't argue the point with me.

With Holly in the back of the Chevy and Victoria beside me I headed along the road. In the rear-view mirror I watched Ruth Beckerman's body grow smaller. Eddie was standing, hands in pockets, looking down the road towards the house. He seemed to have shut the psychiatrist out of his mind so I did the same.

'Any ideas where he might be heading?' I asked.

Holly didn't answer and I glanced over my shoulder. Tears were streaming down her face. She saw me looking and made an attempt at drying the flood. 'I never suspected, never thought . . . My God, I've known him for three years. How could I not know?'

Victoria reached over the back of her seat and took Holly's hand. 'He's had ten years to bury all this,' she said. 'He's been good at it. He fooled his own father, the police, everyone who knew him.'

'But I'm his wife.'

I could have been cynical and told her that wives or husbands are always the last to know about murderers in the family but I didn't. She had enough to worry over for the next few years and wisecracks were not the way to help her do it.

We had the highway in sight now and I slowed and repeated the question.

'We have our own house, we don't use it much but he could have gone there.'

I followed her directions and soon we

were winding down a long narrow road. From the grass growing along its centre, it was clearly seldom used. Water glistened ahead in the early morning sunshine. My eyes felt gritty with lack of sleep.

'The house is on the lakeside,' Holly said. 'You'll see it from the next bend.'

I slowed the car and cruised to a stop at the bend.

The house was ornately rustic with timber and stone the most-used materials. Beyond the house Lake Berryessa stretched calm and untroubled.

A large grey car stood outside the house and Holly, leaning forward, pointed at it. 'He's here,' she said.

Carefully, I engaged reverse and backed up the road a few yards until we were out of sight of the house. 'Is there another way out by car?' I asked.

'No.'

Well, he wouldn't get past the Chevy on this narrow road so if he went at all he'd go on foot. Unless . . . 'Do you have a boat?' I asked Holly.

'Yes, over there in the creek.'

'I'll check the boat first,' I said. I opened the car door and slid out.

Victoria was climbing out too.

'You stay here,' I said.

'Mace,' she said, warningly.

'Okay,' I said. 'I know you're a big girl now, but it only takes one of us.'

'Be careful,' she said.

I hesitated, clasping her hand in mine. 'We could leave this to Collis and his men. It isn't our concern any more.'

'Yes it is,' she said quietly.

I didn't argue. I went into the trees that crowded the side of the road and forced my way through until I was able to find a clear route down to the creek.

I had a good view of it for the last fifty yards and I was sure no one was at the boat, a small but powerful-looking green and white painted launch. When I reached it I took my time checking the exterior before risking stepping aboard. I'd been right, Cliff Monahan wasn't there.

The engine had all the usual bits and pieces that a car engine has and I could have immobilised it in any one of half a dozen ways but I decided to be smart. I left the engine alone and poked around until I found the sea-cocks. I opened them and water bubbled in. Then I clambered back onto dry land and headed down the creek until I reached the lake shore.

Keeping low and using spiky clumps of grass as my cover I worked my way towards the house. From this angle I could see the Chevy but there was no sign of either Victoria or Holly.

A wooden walkway came down to the water's edge from the verandah which surrounded the house.

It was quiet, peaceful; the only sound came from birds calling instructions to one another across the still water.

The gunshot was a heart-stopping crack, made louder by the stillness and my tension which until then I hadn't noticed. Behind me I heard birds clattering up into the sky, their wings beating a staccato retreat. By then I was on the walkway and running for the house, my body bent low, my gun clasped tight in my hand.

25

I slid to a stop, hard up against the stone wall of the house and at that moment I heard another shot from inside. I was close to a window and risked a quick look inside. The room was filled with riding gear and fishing tackle. There were no people in sight.

A few yards along was a door and I was through it and inside before I gave myself time to think about playing safe. Until I knew who was shooting at whom I couldn't sit back. Even if Victoria was a tough, professional cop and could take care of herself I couldn't take chances.

The tack room was separated by a glass-panelled door from a large, high-ceilinged living-room furnished sparsely but with taste. A long window looked down towards the expanse of lawn that bordered the house on the side remote from the creek. At the far end of the room, tucked into the corner between the end of the window and the wall was a bar. Crouched against the bar was Holly. She looked terrified. I couldn't see anyone else.

I eased the connecting door open a crack. Holly saw the movement For an instant her panic stretched even further but then she regained control and pointed a cautious hand to her left. I slipped through the door, and could now see the room was even bigger than I'd thought. A further area, a couple of steps lower, housed a long dining table, hand-carved chairs and a baby grand piano. The piano was the only garish touch. It was painted Hollywood white.

I moved further into the room and then I saw Victoria.

She was standing against the wall, looking into a corner of the room still hidden from my sight. I could see blood on her dress.

I was moving forward, intent on going to her when she spoke. Not to me, she hadn't seen me yet; she was talking to Cliff Monahan.

'You don't want to hurt Holly again,

Cliff,' she said, her voice steady and pitched low. 'She won't harm you.'

I glanced back at Holly and now saw there was blood on her too. A stripe of bright red ran along one forearm. The blood on Victoria must have come from there. I was sorry Holly was hurt but I felt relief that Victoria was unharmed. So far.

'I don't *want* to kill her,' Cliff's voice came from closer than I'd expected. He must be tucked tight in the corner of the room just ahead of me. 'I have to do it. I know I'll die now. Ruth can't save me any more.' He didn't sound crazy. In fact his voice was calm. He sounded as though he was talking to himself. Suddenly there was a sound as he moved along the floor, coming closer to me. 'I'm sorry Holly,' he said. 'I have no choice. I have to spare you what I felt when Laraine . . . Laraine . . . '

'Stay where you are, Cliff,' Victoria said.

I looked at her and now she knew I was there. Her gun, clasped firmly in two hands according to the manual, drooped fractionally. I realised that if Cliff made a move towards Holly Victoria would be unable to shoot because I was in the firing line.

I had to make a fast decision. I shot a glance at Victoria, hoped she interpreted correctly, and went around the corner low and hard and ready for anything.

Cliff Monahan was facing me, his friendly smile in place, his gun held casually and without threat. I realised that had she wanted to do so Victoria could have shot him at any time but must have decided there had been enough killing.

'I'm sorry I shot at you at Karen's house,' he said to me as if apologising for inadvertently stepping on my toe. 'I've already told the Lieutenant how sorry I am that I tried to kill her. Ruth told me I had to do it, you know.' There was another quality in his smile, one that hadn't been present when I'd spoken to him on other occasions: a curiously manic gleam in his eyes that spoke of long suppressed but now raging insanity.

'Give me the gun, Cliff,' I said.

He looked down at the gun in his hand, then slowly shook his head. 'I can't. I have to help Holly. I really must do it.

When I die she will be so sad. I can't let her suffer.'

'There's no need for you to die.'

'Oh, I have to.' There was a childish earnestness about him now. 'Ruth told me what it's like in those places where they send people like me. What they will do to me. The electric shocks. Cold water baths. Strait-jackets. I've seen them in the movies. Ruth showed them to me. I couldn't stand that, you know.'

'It isn't like that, Cliff. Ruth lied to you.'

He frowned, as if chiding me for suggesting Ruth Beckerman could do such a thing. Then he stiffened his shoulders and the gun began to come up.

Behind me Holly screamed. I kicked out, catching Cliff on the elbow as he lifted the gun. He yelled with pain, the gun spiralled into the air and I grabbed for it.

'Cliff, no!' Victoria yelled.

Spinning around I saw he was making a dive for Holly. I tossed his gun towards a couch but held onto my own. I went after him as he reached his wife. He had her short blonde hair in his hands and was pulling her upright. She was screaming at him, trying to fight him off with her uninjured arm.

I hit him on the side of the head with the barrel of the gun and he fell away, his grip loosening. I took hold of Holly, gently so as not to hurt her any more and turned to pass her into Victoria's care. Then I heard Cliff's footsteps as he ran towards the door I'd entered by.

'Let him go,' I said. 'He won't get far.'

I left Holly with Victoria and went outside. Cliff Monahan was running along the lake shore, retracing the path I'd taken in coming up to the house from the creek. I followed, walking, knowing there was no hurry.

He reached the green and white power boat before I was halfway there. I heard the engine start up, cough, die, then burst into full-throated life. I was surprised he'd bothered to start the engine, he must have seen the boat was waterlogged. Unless I'd been too clever. I started running.

I saw the boat slide forward towards

the mouth of the creek. I couldn't see Cliff. As I reached the point where the creek entered the lake the boat accelerated in a burst of foaming water. I yelled, meaningless words which he wouldn't be able to hear anyway. I raised my gun, then dropped my arm to my side. He would be caught.

The boat roared away, then, as I watched, it began to sink lower in the water.

I watched and waited. The boat was sinking fast.

By now it was more than a hundred yards from the shore and still travelling quickly but the engine was labouring. Now, for the first time, I could see Cliff. He must have been crouched low in case I'd fired at him. He was looking shorewards but not at me.

I looked to my right and on the wooden walkway that led down from the house I could see Victoria and Holly. I looked back at Cliff and he had raised a hand as if in farewell.

Then the boat was lower still in the water. Suddenly the motor cut and as silence flowed over the lake once more the boat disappeared in a churning gout of foam.

I waited as the water calmed slowly, expecting to see Cliff's head break water. It didn't.

I started back towards the little pier, yelling questions which Holly couldn't possibly hear from this range. When I reached her it was a waste of time anyway. There were no other boats here.

I stood on the walkway with my arm around Victoria. Then I placed my other arm around Holly and felt her tremble as tears flowed.

I looked at the lake's surface. The wind was getting up and now there were flecks of white where before it had been millpond calm.

'Maybe it's the best thing that could have happened,' I said.

26

Sam Monahan's hospital room had enough people in it to make it a health hazard.

Before Victoria and I finally managed to slip away we had witnessed two scenes of familial togetherness. First, Sam and Holly had helped one another to make their initial adjustments to what had happened. It wouldn't be easy for either of them, learning to live with the fact that Cliff had killed fifteen people and, if he hadn't been stopped, would have extended the list. But they'd made a start, although how long Holly would stick around was debatable. Her career, already on an upswing, couldn't help but enjoy a boost from the publicity these events would attract. Who knows, she might even get to play herself in a movie of all this bloodshed. No doubt someone would come up with that bright idea before many days had passed.

The other scene wasn't exactly family because the relationship between Sally and Andy Morgan and Sam was tenuous to say the least. But Sam needed help and I had the feeling that Sam Monahan's future plans for Laronne would include Sally and Andy.

We said our goodbyes to the Monahans and the Morgans and promised to send the car back when we had picked up Victoria's. Sam wanted me to keep it but it still had a bullet scrape from the hijack and I didn't want reminding.

In the corridor leading towards the hospital exit Sally Morgan caught up with us. 'I feel guilty about Cliff,' she said. 'After all, I was married to him. Maybe something that happened in our relationship pushed him. Maybe I should have seen warning signs.'

'You can't take any blame,' Victoria told her. 'Everyone who came in contact with him was fooled. All except Ruth Beckerman, and she only knew because he confessed it all to her.'

'Maybe you're right,' Sally said.

'I am.'

'Have they found him yet?' Sally asked me.

'They're still dragging the lake. Deputy Collis tells me there are strong under-currents. The body could be anywhere by now, the lake's twenty or thirty miles long.'

Sally nodded. 'I know, we swam there when we were married. Cliff saved me once, I was caught by the under-tow but he pulled me out. He was a strong swimmer.'

Back at the Mount View Hotel we packed our bags and checked out, much to the apparent relief of Phil Smeeton, the desk clerk, who could now relax in the comforting knowledge that he would have nothing more dangerous than a ravening horde of journalists to cope with.

With the bags in the trunk of Victoria's car we walked along the street to the Sheriff's office. Collis didn't look too sorry to hear we were moving on either.

'Found him yet?' I asked.

'No, still looking.'

I told him what Sally had said about Cliff being a strong swimmer.

He shrugged. 'Where would he go?'

I couldn't answer that. Instead I told him I was sorry he'd been pulled into it all and had killed Jimmy Paine as a result.

'I'll live with it,' he said without much conviction. He glanced at Victoria and tried a smile. 'I guess we have something in common now, Lieutenant.'

Victoria nodded her head, her expression sombre. I had a lot of work to do to clean out the guilt she would always feel at the killing of Peter Raskin.

In the Buick she started the engine, then glanced at me with a smile that was not much more successful than Collis's had been. 'Where to?' she asked.

I gave her directions and about an hour later we were descending the hill into Vidal.

'Here?'

'No one will look for us here,' I said. 'No newspaper men or TV crews or police officers or anyone else for that matter.'

'Where do you plan to stay? I'm too old to sleep in the car.'

'You'll never be too old,' I told her.

'For sleeping in cars I'm already too old.'

'How about this place?' We were passing the boarded-up hotel.

'My God, it's probably filled with rats.'

'Let's ask Bill Haigh.'

The old man was on the forecourt of his filling station with a toolkit. The sour expression on his face turned into a smile when we pulled up.

'If you want gasoline I can't help you. The damned pump finally quit on me. If you want anything else you're welcome.'

'How about a room at the hotel?' I asked.

He looked from me to Victoria, then up the street at the hulk of his hotel. Taking off his baseball cap he scratched his round bald head. 'I can't recommend it.' He looked at me carefully. 'You really want some place to stay around here?'

'Definitely.'

'Well, somebody else decided to leave town. I bought up their place. It's not much but there's heat and light.' He grinned. 'They pulled out just yesterday so for all I know the beds might even be warm. But I expect I can rustle up clean sheets.'

The newly vacated house was small but clean and most of the furnishings had been left behind on a promise from Bill to send them on when the former owners were settled.

I carried the bags inside, closed and locked the door and took Victoria in my arms. 'From here on, we talk of nothing but us,' I told her.

'Yes, sir,' she said with a meekness that didn't fool me for a moment.

'Suppose we find out if the beds really are still warm?'

'I thought you'd never ask.'

The bedroom was tiny and comfortable and I don't know how warm or otherwise the bed was because the room had a thick Indian rug on the polished hardwood floor and we settled on that without needing to discuss the matter.

Naked and relaxed where it mattered, and excited where it was needed we made up for the time we had lost chasing our tails over the hills around Calistoga.

'When we are married,' Victoria said

about an hour later, 'I will expect this kind of treatment every day.'

'Optimist.'

'And if I ever see you look at another woman the way you looked at Holly Monahan, I will bite this off.' She gave me a demonstration.

I yelled quietly so as not to disturb Bill Haigh and any of Vidal's inhabitants who hadn't yet left town.

We made love again. Later, bathed and dressed, we went out to find what Bill Haigh had in his pantry. He was nowhere around so we walked down to the lake. It was late afternoon now and the sun was dropping fast towards a range of hazy blue hills beyond the other shore.

Not far away was the cabin where we had found Gil Raskin. I wondered if he and Karen would find some way to salvage a little out of the mess she was in. Perhaps they would. Most of the other people who had survived looked set for levels of happiness. Except Jane Cole, who would probably go downhill fast. Even Markowitz and his cronies would soon be out on the streets and plying their dubious trade and I expected they would find a kind of happiness in that.

The line of cabins began petering out. There were only a couple more and beyond them the black oaks thickened and came all the way down to the shore.

'Let's go back,' I said.

'And do what?'

I took her in my arms again and kissed her. 'Three guesses.'

'Three?'

'I told you before, I'm inventive.'

We turned.

Cliff Monahan stood there.

He was dressed as he had been when I chased him from his house but now his clothes were filthy and he had no shoes on. His hair was matted with dirt and the friendly smile he'd always worn was gone. In his hands he held a rusty woodman's axe with a badly split handle.

My mind raced. I didn't have a gun with me; I had returned it to Sam Monahan's armoury. I had just embraced Victoria and I knew that for once she was unarmed too.

'Hello, Cliff,' I said.

337

He stared at me as if I were a stranger, then he smiled but now it was a wild, ravaged smile. He pointed the axe at Victoria. 'I have to kill you both,' he said. 'I'm sorry, but Ruth told me what will happen to me if I don't.'

'Ruth's dead, Cliff.'

He frowned. 'Ruth?'

'That's right. So you don't have to do anything that you don't want to do ever again.'

He looked from me to Victoria and back again. 'You're lying. Ruth warned me about people telling me lies.' He took a lurching step forward.

I pushed out a stiff arm, thrusting Victoria away from me towards the water's edge. Then I was taking two fast steps forward. There should have been a third forward step but my foot caught in a root of a tree where it knotted up out of the earth. I went sprawling forward and as I did so I saw the rusty axe swinging towards me, the back of the blade thick and heavy and coming straight at my head and there was nothing I could do to stop it.

The blade hit me across the cheekbone and I was thrown sideways with the impact and before I hit the ground I was blacking out.

Desperately, I clung onto consciousness. I heard Victoria cry out and I forced my eyes open. She was backing into the water of the lake. Cliff Monahan was advancing towards her, trailing the axe's blade in the rippling water.

I stumbled after him but it was like a slow-motion replay of some old horror movie. My limbs were not responding to my brain's instructions.

Then Cliff swung the axe up into the air and in that same instant Victoria fell backwards into the water. I heard her scream, a dreadful piercing cry that echoed around my brain.

The axe was now high in the air and the setting sun touched it, turning the rust into golden red. Then it was falling and Victoria, scrambling in the water which churned around her, screamed again.

I lunged forward, suddenly able to move normally, and as I did so an ear-shattering explosion came from close behind me and with it Cliff Monahan's head disappeared in a haze of wet red fragments.

I ran on, into the water. Monahan's body had fallen on top of Victoria and I heaved it aside. The axe handle stood up above the water, the blade buried beneath the surface. I pulled at Victoria's body, lifting her from the water. The axe toppled slowly into the red-stained water beside Monahan.

Victoria was covered in blood, turned pink by the water that had covered her. I couldn't see whether the blood was hers or his.

I turned and carried her out of the lake to lay her gently on the shore.

Bill Haigh stood there, his shotgun, cracked open now, resting in the crook of his one arm. He didn't speak.

Now I could see fresh blood oozing from Victoria's side as I ripped away her sodden dress. A deep gash gleamed red and I could also see something smooth and white. The blow had cut her down alongside her ribcage, but, so far as I could see it had not broken through

I picked her up, unaware of weight or any feelings except one of desperate urgency.

'I'll get the jeep,' Bill said and ran awkwardly ahead of me.

The distance we had walked wasn't far but it seemed like miles and I was relieved when Bill, red faced and breathless raced back to meet me, his battered old jeep, still painted in its wartime camouflage bouncing over the uneven ground.

He turned the jeep behind me and stopped alongside then helped me lower Victoria gently onto a torn bench seat. As we headed for the road which would lead up into the highway Bill fumbled with a radio. 'Goddamn thing,' he muttered. 'Guy I bought this from told me how it works but I'll be damned if I . . . '

I stopped listening because Victoria had opened her eyes. 'Hold on,' I said. 'We'll be at the hospital before you know it.'

She smiled.

I heard Bill talking and realised he had made contact with a Breaker who was responding to a real-life emergency just like they do in the movies.

'An ambulance will meet us,' Bill told me, glancing over his shoulder. 'It's on its way from St Helena now.'

'Thanks, Bill,' Victoria said. 'How'd you like to give a girl away at her wedding?'

Bill managed a grin before looking back at the road ahead. 'I hope you know, young feller,' he said to me out of the side of his mouth, 'that you have yourself one hell of a woman there.'

I looked down at Victoria and touched her face with my fingertips. Her eyes were closed again but I could see a faint pulse beating in the soft flesh of her throat.

I rested a hand carefully against the gash in her side. Blood still flowed but it was much less than before. Leaning down, I kissed her close to the wound tasting her blood on my lips. I tried not to think how close she had come to death.

We were on the main highway now and even above the clattering racket made by the jeep's worn-out engine I could hear the faint spiralling whine of an ambulance siren.